BRUTUS

ON THE RIVER

TEO SPENGLER

ISBN 978-1-7328838-2-6

This is a work of fiction. Names, characters, places, and incidents are either the products of the author's imagination or are used fictitiously. Any resemblance to actual persons, living or dead, businesses, companies, events or locales is entirely coincidental.

Printed in the United States of America
Deeper Dreams Publishing
San Francisco, CA 94121
deeperdreamspublishing@gmail.com
www.teospengler.com

First Printing, 2020

REVIEWS OF BRUTUS, ON THE RIVER

"Teo Spengler covers an enormous swath of emotional territory in this otherwise compact and often gentle novel. On the surface, Brutus is a tale of relationships—both human and animal—set against the backdrop of recent disaster, and Spengler deserves credit for giving readers such a large cast of fully-imagined characters. Beneath the waters, Brutus is an evocative testament to the spirit of survival and a paean to the power of loyalty."

—Jacob Appel

(author, poet, bioethicist, physician,
lawyer and social critic)

"On the River is an amazing and astonishing novel, lyric and painful."

—Susan Griffin

(author, poet, essayist, playwright
and radical feminist philosopher)

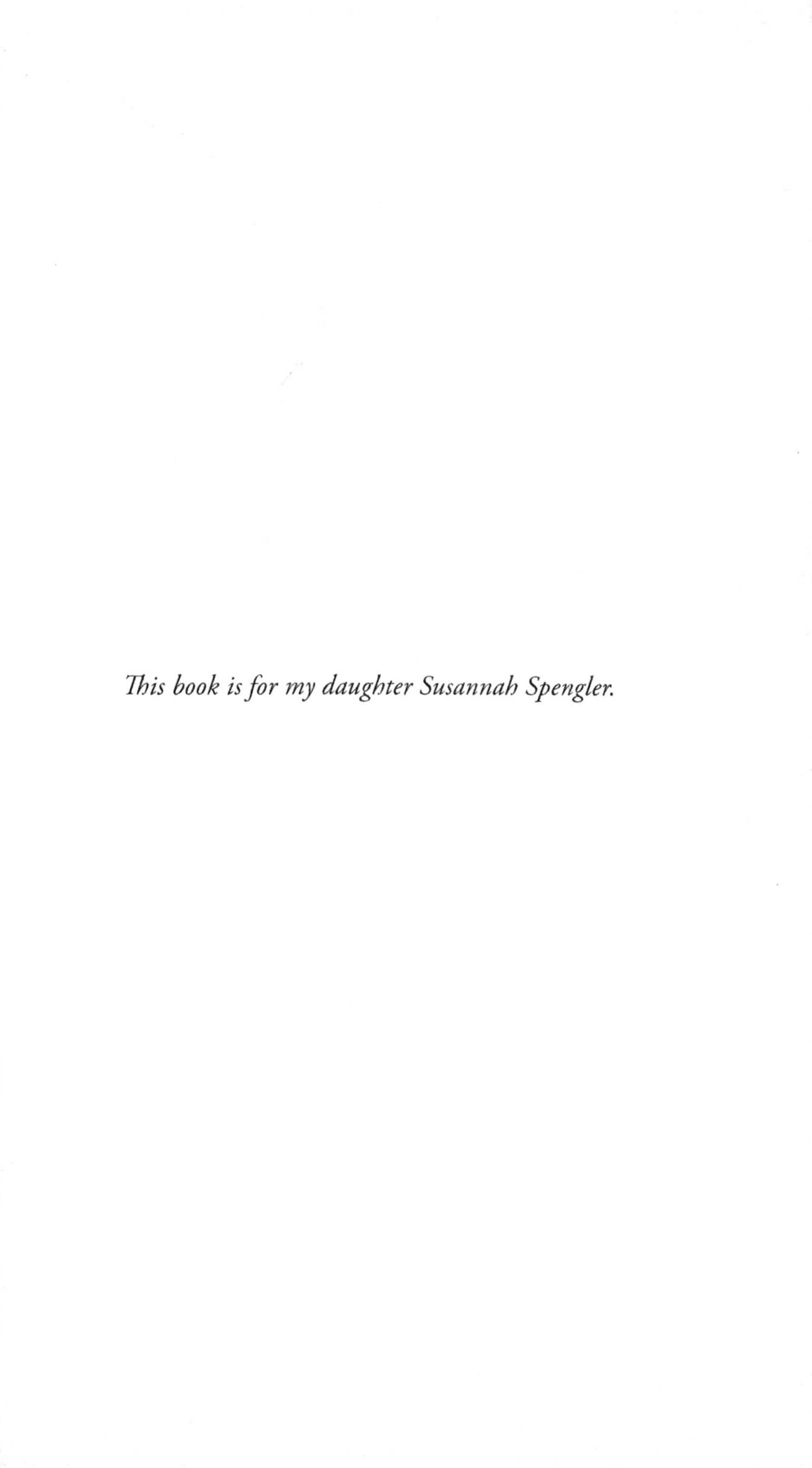

This book is for my daughter Susannah Spengler.

CHAPTER 1

I CAME ONTO THE river after the worst flood in its history. It was springtime, and cleanup had begun or was about to begin. Everything was muddy and damaged, and many fragile things were lost forever.

I rented a small cabin in a double row of cabins. Five cabins faced four others across a garden patio that ran long and thin between them. The garden was gone, the flowering bushes bony and bare, but the redwood sign atop the entryway trellis remained: Garden Court. Vines had covered the trellis before the flood. They were all dead now, stunned then drowned by the overpowering intrusion, and the thin vine fingers still clasped the trellis so tightly they would break if you tried to remove them. You had to pass through that trellis every time you entered Garden Court.

A high wooden fence guarded the cabin complex, but it had not helped at all to keep the river out. The rising, silt-brown water took no notice of it, first passing under it and, later, spilling over the top. Eight of the nine cabins had been completely submerged. The ninth had floated away and it had to be towed back. It was the last in the row. Mine was next to last.

My cabin had been hastily cleaned and repaired. The inner surfaces were freshly white but there was no mistaking that something had happened. The damp smell overpowered the air freshener, and if you leaned against the walls, they made a hollow squishing sound.

A team of repairmen still worked on the other cabins. I saw them carrying sheetrock up the footpath, two men to a board. They muttered *morning ma'am*, and eyed my body when I passed, but otherwise kept to themselves.

The three cabins across the footpath from mine sat on a raised wooden deck. At lunch break the workmen would sprawl on this deck and exchange stories about the devastation. A short, gruff man named Doug was in charge. He liked to play with the two Husky puppies from next door and sang little songs to them. When the men teased him about it and called him Dougy-Wougy, he told them, "Lick it off my zipper."

The two puppies belonged to the people who lived behind my cabin on the other side of the high fence, several women with children and a dozen men. The workers said they were Mexicans. My cabin was built into the fence so I could see their yard through my back window. On Sundays, the men would use the yard between the fence and their house as a place to get together. They would play mariachi music on their car radios and sit in the cars or on the cars and drink beer. Their yard was filled with old cars but none of them ran. The men would line up at Fourth and Main in the early morning to ride in the back of a truck to the vineyards.

The men kept the mother dog tied on a rope behind the house, but the puppies ran free. Mornings they would slide into the courtyard near my cabin through a gap in the fence boards. One was fuzzy yellow and spunky with confidence. The other was softer, smaller, brown and shy. I called them Butterball and Wimpy. The workmen patted both of them and fed them scraps.

Another dog lurked in Garden Court that spring. A skeletal pit bull snatched up whatever food the puppies left. It seemed to live in the cabin complex, but no one claimed it and it spent the afternoons lying uneasily in the footpath. The skin on its rump looked raw and mangy and scars marked its neck. "The Brute," the workmen called it. The dogcatcher came after it several times, but the animal would slink through the gap in the fence into the Mexicans' yard and disappear.

The tenants returned to the cabin across the footpath from mine a few days after I moved in. It was one of the three small cabins built on the deck. From my kitchen window I saw a man and a woman carrying boxes up the stairs to the deck. The woman was stocky and wore a shapeless purple sweater that hung loose over her broad belly. She smoked a cigarette and scowled. The man was lanky with dark hair and beard and he looked young, very young.

I saw them again the next day. The woman wore open-toed Birkenstock shoes with white socks, graying trousers and the same royal purple sweater draping long over her squared hips and belly. She pushed up the sleeves of the sweater but a cuff gave way, covering her wrist and most of one small fist. She shoved it up impatiently. As she bent to lift a box, her sleeve slipped down again. It had a hole worn in the elbow.

When I left my cabin in the afternoon, carefully locking the door behind me, the woman was still moving things in. She glanced at me, put the box she was carrying on a bench near the door of her cabin, and took a cigarette out of a pack in her pocket. She walked toward me, inspecting me as she came. She was quite short, and she marched on her stubby legs with the intense determination of a young child.

"Hi, I'm Shae," she said. Her hair hung to her shoulders, limp on top and ratty below, brown, parted in the middle. The stark lines emphasized the lines of her heavy, square-jawed face and bright, wondering eyes like a kitten.

"Why on earth would you want to move here?" she asked me. "I mean now, of all times?"

I watched as Shae fumbled in a trouser pocket for her cigarette lighter. What to tell her? There was no explaining it. Things had gone wrong, very wrong, rotting from the inside out, and I had come. I reached for words like retreat or sabbatical but had a sudden image of a broken dog crawling to the woods to die.

As it turned out, no response was necessary. Shae was not listening for a reply. She lit the cigarette and continued quickly with her own story. "We lived here before the flood," she said. "I lost everything.

"Larry moved my TV to the top of the refrigerator when we left, and my other good stuff. Moved it up high. The water was only waist deep then. I never thought it might get worse, I just never thought of it. I lost my books, my papers, food in the cabinets. Thank God the stuff from my mum's estate was in storage. I lost everything else."

The man materialized behind her silently. The dark hair and beard cast his face ghostly pale, like a thin cloud in a sunless sky. He was tall but slight, insubstantial, his strong perfect teeth out of place in his fragile face. He remained a few feet behind Shae, closer to their door.

"This is Larry." She turned slightly and gestured toward him with her cigarette. "I was just telling her how I lost everything."

"We got your car out," he offered.

"Hah!" she barked. "A lot of good it does." Shae rolled her eyes and scowled. "Where am I supposed to go?"

There was the river, slow, steady, powerful. It began far away to the east and ended in the Pacific Ocean a few miles past the town. Along the way somewhere the river must have sparkled, silver water laughing and dancing over shiny rocks like in fairy tales. But in town the river flowed dark and somber, smelling of mud and sewage and small things that had died. River Road ran beside it to the ocean, both river and road set deep between small rounded hills.

In town, the river valley broadened, and two streets flanked River Road on each side. First and Second ran beside the river. Then came River Road, then Third and Fourth. That was it. After Fourth Street was a dirt alley, and Garden Court stretched long from one to the other.

There was a cafe in town, at the east end of Third Street where it T-ed into Carlington Woods Road. It had been flooded out. When it reopened, the cafe displayed photographs of the flood. One was a large aerial view of the town under water. Others showed the rescue boats, livestock on roofs, floating debris. People would stop by and look for their friends and their houses in the photographs.

If you did not know anyone in the photos, all you saw was a cold, churning river, gray water swelling its banks, muddy water dispassionately rising, sweeping before it almost by accident everything small, delicate or on the loose. Most of the houses remained, but they were left dirty and empty inside, bereft of their wholeness and purpose, like the standing bush trunks stripped of their leaves. My own emptiness blended smoothly into the landscape of desolation. It was for that, perhaps, that I had come.

The people in the photographs were all trying to get away with a few precious things or with nothing. Their faces were loose like drunks and the only smiles were shiny, shallow smiles. The sandbags had done no good at all. The water swept them away quickly, irreparably. There was no fighting back against the rising tide; there was only the strength to stumble away.

When I returned to the cabin, Shae sat on a chair on the deck drinking coffee. She had finished moving things for the day. She waved me down, squinting into the cool sunlight.

"You'd think they'd do a decent repair job," she said. Then she curled her tongue out and up toward her nose, preparing to speak again. "I mean they got all this insurance money," she said. "It floods every three or four years and they get their fifty thou. Of course, they don't bother to fix the places up. When I plugged in my vacuum, the wall started hissing at me."

Shae was going to a friend's house to take a bath. She spoke the word *bath* with the soft Boston "a". I saw her later, trudging down the footpath carrying a little leather overnight case. Scowling, she circled wide around the wary pit bull and was gone.

The cabins did not have baths. They had small shower-stalls and sinks. The sink in my cabin fell off the wall the first time I tried to turn it on. It looked strange on the floor, not like a sink at all. I told the man Doug about it, but he said the repair crew had finished my cabin. If something went wrong, it was for the maintenance crew to fix. The maintenance crew had only one man since everyone else had been hired away. They said he had no experience. He put my sink back on the wall though and it still ran water. Many houses in the hills remained without running water.

The local newspaper carried an article about a woman who was raped by four locals. She lived in the hills and hitchhiked to town to get water. They picked her up on her way back. One after the other, the men raped her. She said she was not angry, just tired. That she would not open her legs to a man for a long, long time. That she would live alone forever.

That night as I lay on my mattress trying to sleep, a man took water from the hose tap in front of my cabin. I heard a noise outside my window and saw his head and shoulders, dark against dark through the pane. I turned on the cabin light and saw with clarity my own reflection in the window glass. I switched it off quickly, blinding myself.

After a while I went outside with a flashlight and found the hose outlet still running. The man was gone. Only the mangy pit bull was there, in the doorway of the next cabin, curled tight on the welcome mat against the cold night. He glanced up, the whites of his eyes showing.

CHAPTER 2

I DID NOT SEE the boy move into the last cabin between my cabin and the alley; one day he was just living there. Shae said that his name was Michael, that he had lived on the River before the flood but not in Garden Court. He was very beautiful, sturdily built with soft blond hair to his shoulders and the clear distant eyes of an archangel. His was the smallest cabin, the one that had floated away in the flood, and he stayed in it most of the time.

A weeping willow shaded the area between my cabin and the boy's cabin. Its trunk was solidly rooted near the fence, but its shadow was alive, fluid, influencing the entire area between the two cabins. The leafy pattern on the weather-aged picnic table changed with every breath of wind. My kitchen door opened to that mix of sun and shade, but the boy's cabin had neither door nor window on that side and he rarely came out. Sometimes I would feel his presence behind his cabin wall.

One afternoon he appeared in his doorway standing

tall and downy, naked to the waist, perfectly sculpted. "I dreamed there was another flood," he announced.

Shae stopped in her tracks on the deck, ten feet from the boy's door. "Don't even say that," she barked.

The boy's eyes were pale blue. He directed them at Shae. As she spoke, he withdrew them into himself without turning them away from her until they were completely withdrawn. At that point, he backed into his cabin, closing the door behind him.

"I was going to bring some things from my mum's estate out today, but I think I'll wait," Shae said. "I have a lot of faith in Michael's dreams."

It did rain that night. Late in the evening, clouds edged in from the west bloodying the sunset sky. I watched their progress from behind my kitchen window. On the other side of the window was a bare thorn bush. It had been very beautiful before the flood, Shae told me, with lush leaves and delicate white roses. It had looked to the rain clouds for sustenance but met betrayal. I sat at the window as long as I could, keeping the bush company into the night.

The rain stopped by morning. I stepped around puddles on my way to the cafe. I walked the four blocks to the cafe every morning early. Even when I awoke on the mattress on the floor of my cabin, shaken by the dark dreams I could not remember, the thought of the cafe filled my mind. As I slipped on jeans, I was already experiencing the cool purposefulness of the walk, past the little houses, past the old Victorian converted to the Mental Health Center, past the Bordeaux Veterinary Clinic, the diesel yard on the right and the open field on the left, a right turn then left to Carlington Woods Road. I would smell the warmth of the coffee as I entered, surveying the empty tables with relief, safe in the knowledge that for an hour or so I could be there.

I read the local paper every morning carefully. I read each article, each page: the police blotter, the report on how to sign up for federal natural disaster aid, the speculation on whether the big city upriver caused the flood by opening its own flood gates. I got my free refill, then read the comics, the classifieds, the list of missing pets, the freebie column. When I was done, I left and walked back to the cold cabin planning in my mind what to do next and after that. There was not much to do, sweep the cabin, walk around the block. On Sundays the paper was bigger, and I could stay in the cafe for several hours.

One Sunday when I returned to Garden Court late morning, Shae was on the deck in front of her cabin. She was standing books in neat rows to dry in the sun.

"Can you believe it?" she rushed to tell me. "They start construction next door at seven in the morning, even on Sundays! I'm going to call the cops if they do it again. I told them so."

She held a ceramic mug of coffee and she circled first one then the other palm around it. No steam came up from the coffee; a white film floated on top. She sat on a bench drinking the lukewarm coffee and sorting damaged books.

The books were more misshapen than dirty. Shae had packed them in boxes before the flood and the cardboard sifted out some of the mud. They were good titles, many hardbound, but warped by the flood water to the shape of tombstones. I saw *Crime and Punishment*, *In Cold Blood*, John Hawke's *Lime Twig*, some Jerzy Kosinski, books of lawbreakers and predators and crazies. Shae was lining them up in an orderly fashion, row after row of standing, swollen books. The deck looked like a little graveyard.

"I think I can save some of these once the sun dries them off." Shae watched me inspect a Cervantes bloated beyond recognition. My hand could not span it. The sun filtered cool through the redwoods. "Well," she said. "What do I have to lose?"

The loss itself was staggering. You could not get away from it; everywhere you went, there it was. As the town was set in the river valley, each house in the bowl of the town was gutted, each shop a total loss. I walked at ease through the desolation, camouflaged by the rot and ruin, like a brown Rock Lizard on a brown rock wall. It was for this that I had come.

After the first few weeks, people came back weekends to inspect their ruined possessions and to make certain nobody stole any. Once I went across the bridge and up the road on the other side of the River and saw men with shotguns guarding empty, ravaged houses. The men nailed up plywood to close the staring window holes and watched over the remains, sometimes with guard dogs. I did not cross the bridge again that summer; there was devastation enough on my own side of the river.

The next time I saw the boy Michael, he was carrying garbage to the bin in the dirt alley. A gap had been cut into the wooden fence beside Shae's cabin so that you could get through to the garbage bin on the other side. It was some twenty feet from the boy's door.

I was sitting at the picnic table between my cabin and his, feeding the puppies the remains of a sandwich. Michael did not look toward my cabin at all. He walked to the break in the fence, slowly, silently, eyes aimed somewhere far ahead. He deposited the bags, then turned and walked back, his arms long and golden at his sides. The sleeves of his faded T-shirt had been hacked off.

As the boy approached his door, the fluffy puppy ran up to him. It wiggled its body and its brown eyes shown like steely marbles. Michael moved his gaze to me for a long second as if assessing the distance between us, weighing some risk only he could see. Then he leaned over and patted the puppy twice on the head. The smaller puppy followed the first but stood shyly just outside Michael's range. As the boy reached out to it, Shae pushed open her side window with a bang and both pups scuttled away. They wriggled through the hole in the fence next to my cabin. Michael stood up, pondering the fence where the pups had gone.

"The butterball and the wimpy puppy," he said, using my nicknames for the pups. "How can brothers be so different?" He stood silently awhile, lost in some vision of his own.

Finally, he looked up. "So, what is it that is wrong with you?" he asked me sternly.

A breeze came up. I felt the shadow of the weeping willow form and change and form again, dark on my skin. The leaves brushing against each other dryly made a long, sighing sound.

"I don't know," I said. I did not know, nor had all the king's horses and all the king's men been able to tell me. The finest doctors money could buy had found nothing wrong with me. One declared me a perfect specimen of young womanhood and invited me to dinner. But they were wrong, all wrong, so very wrong.

The boy suddenly raised one golden arm, pointing to a spot behind me. I turned and saw the Brute a few feet from me, thick neck and jaws emerging from jutting ribs and rotting pelt. I jumped from my seat and leaped back. The animal retreated, keeping low to the ground, then lunged back desperately to grab the remaining crust. One side of its face was swollen, and its ears were torn.

"The Mexicans fight dogs," Michael said. "They bet on them."

"There's no law you have to believe every racist thing you hear," Shae opined from inside her cabin. Michael went into his house and bolted the door.

On the other side of the garbage bins was the dirt alley. It passed behind Garden Court, then circled back up to connect with Carlington Woods Road in front of the cafe. One day I walked up the alley and stood by the Mexicans' house. I saw the broken cars in the yard, the tall wooden fence, the back of my own cabin. It felt odd looking at my cabin like that, as if I were spying on myself, sneaking up on my own life.

Beyond that yard was a deep, U-shaped driveway leading to another house, a small one with bay windows. Trees backed the home protectively. I walked closer, up the U-shaped driveway. Most of the doors and windows were gone like in a doll house. I peered in and saw a refrigerator and a chair covered with mud. Everything was dirty, covered with mud.

I remembered a dream I had years before. I was running down a dirt road and came upon a large home with nobody there. I walked through the house and found the room of a little girl. It was okay to take anything I wanted because the entire family was dead.

Nobody had died in the great flood. People had lost and lost and lost but nobody had died. The newspaper said the town should be grateful for that. The mortuary was across Fourth Street from Garden Court and even though the mortician repaired his facilities quickly after the flood, he had no business. He would drive the two shiny hearses around the block now and again to keep their engines in shape. The rest of the time he sat on the steps of the mortuary and smoked dope. I smelled it when I walked to Safeway in the afternoons.

One afternoon I walked down the dirt alley, past the Mexicans' house, past the gutted Victorian. Just before the roadway curved up to join Fourth Street, I saw an abandoned park stretching from the alley back to the redwood forest. The part of the park closest to me was a flat grass field, fringed with trees and high bushes. A short, gnarled tree grew in the center of the field, its branches bare. Tramps sat on a dilapidated bench beneath it with dogs at their feet; two men, two dogs. One of the men had a long, pointed beard like a wizard.

"That's Michael and Mickey, the tramps with dogs,"

Shae told me later. "They're harmless. Alkies but okay, not like some other bums around town."

She talked about a group of homeless men who hung around near Safeway, Bear and his gang, definitely bad news. "But Michael and Mickey are okay," she said. "They each have a dog, Mollybelle and Lulabelle; been here for years."

As I sat in the cafe the next morning, I saw them walk by. First the bearded one, Michael, and his dog, headed for the park. He had a tall staff in one hand and carried a paper bag in the other. Within a half hour, the other man and his dog walked by in the same direction. The dogs may have been related, one a sleek, chubby Dalmatian, the other the same shape but with brown and yellow spots. I saw them pass every morning after that, the men carrying their beer cans in little paper bags.

One morning I walked by that park a little later than usual and the first man was already there. His face was long and craggy beneath the beard, deeply lined. He held a can of beer in one hand and seemed to be talking to himself. His dog, the Dalmatian, frisked over to me, wiggling its wide rear.

"Morning lass," the man said. He spoke with a Scottish accent. "Mollybelle won't hurt you. She's just saying hello."

I patted the dog. Her short coat was smooth and sleek as a Chinese carpet. She wore a red collar with two bells on it.

"Okay Mollybelle," he said. His eyes were bright blue. The dog immediately turned and retraced her steps, plopping down on the grass near the man's feet. Her muzzle was open, and it looked as if she were smiling.

I walked out to the tree. The dog rolled on her back laughing.

"I was just talking to this tree," the man said. He drank some beer before he continued, taking his time telling me as if we were old friends. "If you are all alone, lass, if you have no one to talk to, tell your troubles to a tree and the tree will help you. An Indian told me that," he explained, "a Lakota chief. Indians teach that to their children."

I squatted down and touched the dog's silky head. I had had allies and adversaries and admirers, but I had always been alone. None of them could see through the pale skin to the darkness inside me. I looked at the tree. It was an apple tree. Tiny, almost indiscernible buds dotted its branches. The strong, wild scent made me dizzy.

That evening Shae invited me in for a cup of coffee. Her cabin was one small room with the kitchen built into the far wall. Larry lay slumped on the bed watching Columbo on television. With one finger, he stroked his gray cat. It was missing an eye, an ear and its tail. Larry smiled at me sweetly, teeth flashing for an instant, and then he moved over to make room on the bed for me to sit. He was drinking a glass of Coke, pouring from a two-liter bottle. Shae made coffee, then pulled up a folding chair. She talked above the TV.

"So you saw Michael today?" Shae said. "I hear his mum buys all his food for him. That she shops at Safeway for him every Tuesday, then leaves him pocket money that he buys booze with. I've never seen him at a meeting."

I explained that I wasn't talking about young Michael, but it took her awhile to understand. "Oh, *that* Michael,"

Shae said finally, "old Michael, the tramp." She curled her tongue toward her nose, nodding. "I saw him playing his accordion on River Road. People were giving him money too. All these tourists come to gawk at the flood damage. They give him money." She stood up and stubbed out her cigarette in an overflowing ashtray on the kitchen counter. "Of course, he only buys booze with it," she added.

"His dog is cute. That's why people give him money," Larry suggested. "The dog is so cute."

"I should get a cute dog," Shae said. "Maybe people would give me money. Hah!" she snorted, lifting her chin. It was a small chin, despite the layers beneath it, a small chin in a small face but she raised it with an air of defiance.

"Fat chance," she continued. "I'd be happy if they just don't steal anything else. Like my aunts, for example." She pronounced it *ont*.

"Can you believe it, my aunts looting my mum's house before I got there? I mean, society ladies. Of course, they're all alkies, though nobody ever admits it. At my mum's funeral, everyone pretended she died of a weak heart."

Columbo resumed and we all watched the unprepossessing detective track down evidence and piece together the mystery. Larry stroked the battered cat gently. Every now and then he felt for his glass of Coke and took a sip, his gaze never leaving the television. In time his eyes became bright and lively as if he gained energy from the white light that emerged from the screen.

CHAPTER 3

I TOOK A JOB with management, tending the grounds of Garden Court. They asked around first but there were no takers. The pay was low, and everyone found the idea of spraying water on dead plants somehow disturbing. I heard about it and volunteered. It would fill some time.

They bought me a rake, a shovel, and a long hose with a fancy nozzle. The nozzle was metal with a lever like an over-sized trigger to regulate the water flow. If you pressed the trigger lightly, the water sprayed thin and gauzy, white-edged as if with lace. But if you shoved it down as far as it would go, the water came out in a solid, powerful shaft with enough push, the packaging said, to knock a bird out of the sky.

When the trigger was released, the water cut off. The instructions warned the user not to rely on this mechanism to stop the water flow for any extended period. If you forgot to turn the water off at the tap, pressure would build up all night over the length of engorged hose and something had to give. The manufacturer disclaimed liability for any resulting damage.

Something about the warning disturbed me. It was not the disclaimer; I knew it was worthless. I had had one just like it thrown out by the high court. I had worked as a lawyer then – was it only months ago? – but that was a previous life, a life of silk suits and limousines, where words and logic were the only tools I needed, my sword and my magic, and none had used them better. But then logic had failed me, and words could not touch the strangeness inside me, even to give it a name. I looked over the gardening things and doubted if any was the right tool to fix whatever it was inside me that had gone so wrong.

After I was hired, I took stock of the plants in Garden Court. Nothing under three feet had survived. I could only guess at how many small ones there had been before the flood by counting the empty beds.

The big trees towered above the cabins. They had not been affected by the flood; their strength lay within. Muddy water was no threat to big trees on solid ground even when it rose to a level higher than a grown man standing erect. The redwoods, the willow, the oaks–their lives in Garden Court continued unchanged. The great flood was no more than another minor disturbance recorded somewhere beneath their bark in a slight variation of the rings.

The smaller trees and shrubs in Garden Court were my primary charge; without exception, these were blighted. The slender thorn bush outside my window stood about my height. It had survived the flood, but it produced only a few scattered leaves and its bark was lackluster. Something was clearly wrong with it, but it was difficult to say just what it was.

The five tall shrubs that lined the footpath in front of the deck suffered more obvious damage that left their roots exposed, their leaves muddy. Several more bushes huddled beside the deck cabins, bent over with the weight of the caked silt on their branches. The spiky rose bushes just inside the entryway were also in bad shape and the brittle vine on the Garden Court trellis was clearly dead.

I hosed all of these plants down early in the morning before any of the residents came out. By this time most of the cabins were occupied but nobody seemed to get up before noon. Next to Shae and Larry lived a short old woman named Vama who was from Yugoslavia. She had a fear of gas asphyxiation and moved in only after management took out the cook stove and turned off the gas to her cabin. She wore her hair in braids pinned up around her head and she walked slowly, shifting her weight completely to each side with her steps, like a wind-up walking toy. Every week or so she would pack up a suitcase and head down River Road, but someone always brought her back to the little deck cabin. Next to Vama lived Grover, a bedridden man of about ninety years, completely deaf.

After the cluster of small deck cabins was a larger cottage. Another elderly lady lived there with her middle-aged son who was on disability. They said he had flashbacks from the war. The final cabin on that side bordered on Fourth Street; a young woman lived there with her three children, and the smell of hot food lingered outside that door.

Across the footpath from the cooking lady lived a slim-hipped Puerto Rican woman called Felicia. She appeared to be about twenty-five years old, but she had a teenage daughter who lived with the local mortician. Felicia often looked normal but sometimes her face would twist, furrows appearing on her forehead in crazy lines like you never see. At these times, she would nail four or five straw crucifixes to the outside of her cabin door and leave them up for days.

Beside Felicia was the only unoccupied cabin. It looked like the other cabins and had no obvious disadvantages, but it remained empty. After a cluster of redwoods came my cabin; Michael's was the last. I watered it all down several times a week in the early mornings.

One Tuesday morning when I was out working in the yard, a woman walked under the Garden Court trellis flinching a little as if she thought the trellis might fall just as she was passing beneath it. She wore a pale pink dress and carried a matching handbag. When she came to the section of the footpath where the pit bull was sleeping, she clutched her purse to her chest with both arms and pressed her lips together. Then she sidled around the Brute, taking quick, sly steps.

Shae peered out her window. "Look out for that dog!" she called. "Somebody's gonna get hurt one of these days."

I continued spraying the willow tree. The woman nodded a greeting to Shae, but she walked right up to me.

"I'm Michael's mother," she said. As she extended her hand to me, I smelled hairspray and some light perfume. I transferred the hose to my left hand, dried my right one on my jeans, and shook her hand. It was cold and small.

"You must be the young lady attorney," she said. "Mr.

Marcuzi from management told me about you. He was surprised that you wanted to do the garden work, such a pretty girl, and with your credit references! But some people like to garden."

I took my hand back and let it fall loose at my side. The left one held the nozzle out in front of me and cold water leaked onto the palm, sliding down the forearm to the elbow, then dripping down, pooling on the ground. I knew I should say something but being mistaken for normal brought the familiar nausea. Sweat prickled my forehead, and I smelled it, or something, heavy and rancid.

"It's so good to have respectable people here," the woman continued. "Michael needs good influences around him." She sighed and stepped a little closer to me. "I just don't know what to do," she confided. "If only they find the right combination of medicines."

The truth was: I did not know much about plants or their problems. I bought a book in Safeway on plants and read it carefully, but it did little to assist me. The book described various pests that might attack outdoor plants and listed other common plant problems, their causes and their cures. Specific, isolated symptoms were addressed–from wooly white mealy bugs to striated leaves–but the book did not mention a general and drastic decline where the plant displayed none of the normal signs of being alive yet was not dead. The book did not discuss an overwhelming shock to the entire plant system nor did it offer any tips on how to lead such plants back to normalcy.

I noticed a green, living smell around the geraniums in front of the local cafe after the rain, so I sprayed the

Garden Court plants often and packed the earth securely around their roots and tried to clean the River mud off their leaves. This cleaning was not easy. The mud clung to the leaves tenaciously, more like a shadow or a stain, and water alone had no effect. In the end, I scrubbed each leaf separately with an old toothbrush until I could see the vein lines, precise as hieroglyphics on a forgotten tomb.

Not long after I took the gardening job, I saw a dog fight in the Mexicans' yard. When the men congregated there, drinking beer and listening to the radio, they would clap and stomp to the mariachi beat. Their noises seemed a natural part of the music and I did not think much about it until one afternoon the stomping and hooting moved away from the rhythm of the music. Beneath it I could hear the dark roar of animal noises.

I went into my cabin and looked out the back window. In a space between the broken cars, two dogs were fighting, rolling over and over, a snarling mass of teeth and muscle. The larger one was a pit bull, the sharp black-gray color of a shadow at high noon. The other looked like the pup Butterball but bigger, some husky-shepherd mix. As I watched, the dogs broke off to reconnoiter for position, pacing off beside one another, guarding their throats, watching and judging the moment, heads high, backs high, every muscle of their taut bodies straining to get the upper position. The men circled round and smacked the air with their fists, yelping their excitement.

The dark energy of the fight flowed in through the window chilling me instantly to the bone. Before fear could paralyze me, I raised a fist and rapped hard on the glass of the window. The noise shot out strong and the circle of human bodies broke and the human howls stopped abruptly. With the silence I could hear the deep chest growl of the dogs and their deep, desperate sucking in of air. Just as suddenly, the human noises resumed. One man called out something in Spanish, then the others said it, shrugging shoulders, slouching and laughing a little, then laughing more. They threw back their heads to laugh and I could see the teeth, wet and shiny. My fingers began to tremble, but I stayed there, the witness at the window.

As I watched, the shadow dog broke to the side then lunged up and suddenly mounted the other's shoulders, looming over the husky, head above head, looking for a hold. Every fiber of the husky's body reacted instantaneously, and it surged under and up with new strength to throw off the death grip, and the dogs rolled over and over, fighting to rise first, to keep the other from rising. Their low, guttural growls seemed to come from the earth itself.

I forced my body to move, my arm to reach for the phone. I called the police, then read and reread the back blurb of a matchbook to block the fear, my hands thrust deep in my pockets to stop the trembling. When I heard the car in the alley, the voice of authority, I peered out the window again. The fight was breaking up. One of the men stepped over and gave the seething mass of dog a shove with his foot and a second grabbed the husky by the collar and flung it across the yard toward the house. He shoved the dog against the wall and held it there with his knee while he opened a door to the basement level. The two pups scampered out, but the man pushed the husky in and slammed the door. As the police car pulled away, a third man grabbed a shovel and was shooing the shadow dog out of the yard. In that split second, I saw it perfectly, ears cropped close to its wide head, neck thick, chest deep, its compact body tight with layered muscles.

Suddenly the shadow dog turned. The man seemed to move in slow motion and the dog shot past the shovel as though it were not there, streaking around the man, the cars, a smooth black flash across the yard like a hawk's silhouette, and even as the other men were turning, even as I was opening my mouth to scream, the dog grabbed for the littlest puppy. The men rushed it immediately with the shovel and with sticks and the pup rolled on its back in submission, its eyes wide and its tail curled under, but the dog seized Wimpy by the throat. It shook the pup savagely once, twice, then a man hit it with the shovel and it dropped the body and was gone, the men raising their fists and yelling in Spanish after it. The pup did not move. Its neck was snapped.

I couldn't move from the window. I just stood there staring out at the lifeless body, disconnected images flipping crazily through my mind: a sparrow twitching slightly in a man's hand, a red stain on white sheets, moonlight slanting into a dark room, my sister's eyes blank and staring.

On the other side of the window, Wimpy's body lay still between old cars. Finally, one of the men put it in a garbage bag and dumped it in the alley behind Garden Court.

Later, I walked to the abandoned park. The sun was traveling low in the sky leaving streaks of red on the pale clouds.

It was eventide. Soon the streaks would fade and the sky turn luminous blue, gradually deepening in tone as if someone were inserting screens of the same color blue, one after another, between sun and earth. At length, the blue itself would disappear from the sky, leaving only the dark, though not quite the same dark as the trees which would still stand dark against the lighter backdrop. At some point, the sky would become the same color as the trees and hills and all elements would merge into night.

In the dusk, the tramp Michael sat slumped on the bench under the apple tree. He was drinking liquor from a pint bottle, his dog Mollybelle curled at his feet. She rose when she saw me but did not approach. I had wrapped the puppy in a white cloth to bury it. I sat down beside Michael. He had heard the story but he had not believed it: a grown dog will not hurt a puppy. He looked at the little body, then spit fiercely on the ground.

"Son of the river, that shadow dog," he said. "Son of darkness." He peered at me, his face flushed with the drink, his breath heavy with it. "But you know that darkness, don't you lass?" he said. "It's in you, isn't it, and you've come to the River to fight it."

The wind churned the very tops of the trees and the birds wove and twisted their evening calls into an intricate web of song. From the forested part of the park I could hear trees creak in the wind with the same noise old doors make being pushed open. I held the little parcel in my arms. The body was long cold, but it felt warm the way a tree trunk feels warm to a child wrapping thin arms around it to ground her. I felt a power surging just under my skin and I knew I could uproot the tree and fling it across the ocean with one hand.

"Don't go thinking it's easy, child," he said. "Don't go thinking it's easy. Old Man River will break you if he can, the bleeding bastard."

He took another swallow and the anger passed. He sat there slumped on the park bench. His coat was torn, dirty. The smell of gin almost blotted out the scent of the apple blossoms, but not quite. The sweet, wild aroma still lingered on the air.

I could not sleep that night. As I lay there, the strangeness returned, the same symptoms that riddled my life as a lawyer: the racing heart, the constriction like a huge hand squeezing, the chasm of nothingness, and with that sense of distance, the rising tide of panic. I knew where this would take me and fought to contain it. But the puppy's eyes, wide with fear, bored into me, and fear overwhelmed my own defenses like flood water pouring over sandbags. Even when I said aloud that there was nothing wrong with me, even when I listed off all the tests they had done and all the results, my body kept trembling, my heart pounding a frantic warning.

I tried to hold on, staring hard at the light bulb dangling from the ceiling on a cord, but it did not seem real and nothing seemed real. I teetered there on the very edge of reality, now nearer, now farther, as if struggling with some invisible foe, then I was gone, out of my body, plunging fast into the crazy emptiness of thin air.

CHAPTER 4

MORNING CAME, AS always, a little too late. By dawn, nothing had happened. Out my back window, the wrecked cars rusted placidly in the sunshine and the mother dog yawned, and then ate something from her bowl. Only *I* had not passed unscathed; instead of marching briskly to the cafe, I blew along like a dead, dried leaf.

From the safety of the cafe, I turned the episode over in my mind, looking at every angle like the detective Columbo might inspect a bloody shoe at a crime scene, holding it with gloved fingers to the strong light. What had unearthed the craziness inside me this time? I had been doing so well.

It had begun with the dogfight and ended with the dead puppy, the dead puppy Wimpy. The puppy appeared in my mind, eyes wide and scared. It set my teeth chattering and I squeezed my hands around the coffee mug until my fingers ached. Little Wimpy. I saw it clearly now; it was naming the dog that had hooked me. It was an error, an error I would not repeat. No more dogs, no more dogfights.

As soon as I returned to the cabin, I called management to bar up the window. They sent the maintenance man Jack over that afternoon. Jack had dark, wavy hair and a baby face like the leader of a big band. I told him that I wanted solid boards covering the back window. He did the work without curiosity, neither asking for an explanation nor glancing at the contents of the cabin any more than necessary to avoid knocking anything over. In the end he did knock into a stack of boxes, tipping one over, but he did not so much as glance down.

I bolted the door after him and went back to clean up. Books and papers littered the carpet, certificates, awards, a photo with the governor, the rubble of my former life. I had been a good lawyer, better than good, a rising star. I had made a name for myself then left it behind with most of the other trappings of normalcy as the strangeness rose within me and I took off like old Vama, carrying a big suitcase of useless mementos. Here at my feet was a bundle of Supreme Court briefs, there a half dozen books.

A thick book lay on its back split open to a central page–Witkin on Evidence. A photo had been placed there, perhaps to mark some important section although the page meant nothing to me now. The photo was in black and white and showed a young child, a mug shot, head and shoulders framed by a white border as if she were looking out a white-sashed window. The face was clear, the lines precise as the veins of a new leaf. Both front baby teeth were missing. I put the photo back in the book and replaced it in the box.

When I went out again, it was too late to garden. The

shadow of the willow stretched long fingers toward the deck where Shae sat with a pocket calculator and some papers. Her shoulders slumped so low that her body looked oval, like an egg standing upright on one crushed tip. She had forgotten two checks she had written, she told me brightly, tensing her lips as if to smile but not smiling. She would have no money at all until the check next month so there went Larry's birthday.

Shae had hoped to have a party for his birthday, she told me. She had planned to bake a chocolate cake frosted in white. She was going to draw an ocean on top of the cake with a gray bus driving up to it and the words "Happy Birthday Larry" written over the waves.

They had met on a Greyhound bus, she said, and they drank and talked all the way across the country. He was a plumber, he'd told her. He had a high school diploma. He was heading west just to swim in the Pacific Ocean.

"It turned out he couldn't swim," Shae said. She extracted the last cigarette in the pack, but she didn't light it, just flipped it around in her fingers. "He just waded in, then he came back to shore. We laughed and laughed."

They had been happy for a time, but it did not last long. First was the nightmare of his brother escaping from jail and coming after Larry, then Shae's mother died and her aunts stole most everything of value in the house before she could get back east, then her job gave her neck pains so she had to go on disability, then the flood. Now it was his birthday and it was up to her to do something about it. His family was out of the picture, his brother hopefully dead or at least in prison, so who would even remember that it was his birthday? It gave her the chills to think that nobody would remember, as if he didn't really exist at all. It gave me the chills too. It was like that tree that falls in the forest with nobody there to hear. Did something not happen if nobody remembered it? Or did it happen anyway, then unhappen when forgotten? Did unhappening leave a trace? A bloody footprint?

I told Shae that I would give the party. I would buy a cake at the cafe and we would eat it at the picnic table. No dogs were involved. This simple interaction would pass without incident.

The cafe carried cakes by that time, cakes and pastries and other bakery items. In the three months since the flood, it had been renovated unobtrusively, the daily changes too minor to provoke outcry from those who counted on its sameness. They installed a new cooler one week, enlarged the display cabinets the next. The two small windows facing Carlington Woods Road were replaced with one large pane of safety glass. The policemen would sit there and munch pastries and watch for speeders, but I never saw speeders early in the morning. There was only Michael and Mickey with their dogs headed for the park, the young veterinarian, tall and blond as a Ken Doll opening up the clinic, and workmen in old trucks going to some job site. Once I saw the shadow dog run by and I pointed it out to the policemen, but they were not concerned. Male dogs fight, one of the policemen told me; it was in their nature. Department regulations aside, he personally could not fault an animal for acting according to its nature.

The problem with the birthday party was that there was

no one to invite. Larry had two friends, George and Robbie, but they were in AA and would not socialize outside the Program. They had planned a fishing trip with Larry for the morning after his birthday and they would celebrate then. Shae told me to invite anyone at all.

The next day when I was working in the yard, Michael walked out of his cabin. He carried a can of Miller beer, dangling it from the plastic loops that hold a six-pack together. He sat on his front step, yanked off the plastic and tossed it into the footpath. When he popped the can open, it sizzled angrily.

I was loosening the earth beneath the deck-cabin bushes. The plant book said that a certain lightness of soil was essential to allow nutrients to get to the roots, so I was loosening the soil with a short, three-pronged tool that looked like the foot of a big bird. The tool was sharp and cut deeply into the earth. It also cut deeply into my left palm when it got in the way, but I blocked off the pain. It was a trick I knew, imagining that an injured body part was made of wood.

"No more Wimpy," Michael said in a loud voice. I looked over to see who he was talking to, but nobody was there except the yellow puppy. Michael took a long drink of the beer, then smoothed back the pup's ears against its fuzzy head. "Your friend got it, didn't he? Your brother," Michael told the dog. "Thanks to someone who called the cops."

Michael drank some beer. He glared at me as I sprinkled compost over the turned soil and began to work it in. He sniffed loudly, chugged whatever beer remained, then crushed the can with one hand. I remembered his arms from the first time I saw him, young and golden, but when I turned around to look, he was wearing a long-sleeved Mickey Mouse sweatshirt. His eyes again took on the stern regard of an archangel, but he could not possibly judge me more harshly than I judged myself.

"He tried to run but he just couldn't make it," Michael said to the puppy. "We better practice up, pup. Who knows what she'll do next?"

I stood up and knocked the claw against the deck to clean it. My left hand was still bleeding so I kept it behind me as I turned to Michael.

"I'm having a party," I told him. "For Larry's birthday."

Michael forgot about the puppy and stared at me, hard and unblinking. "You really are crazy," he said. It was clear that he had toyed with the idea but never expected immediate confirmation.

Michael nodded to himself, still watching me closely. "They come and take you away if you are crazy," he said. At this his gaze changed and he withdrew the focus with dizzying swiftness until he seemed miles away, shaking his head from side to side almost imperceptibly. He rose cautiously to his feet and then backed to his cabin and went in quickly. I heard him throw the bolt lock behind him.

The locks on the doors of the Garden Court cabins were good bolt locks. I asked about it before I moved in and management assured me that the locks were new, with solid steel throws that passed two full inches into the door frames themselves. When they were fully extended, the pins locked solidly into place. Management demonstrated this, opening the cabin door and flipping the bolt so that I could see it extend straight and stiff. It locked into place with a metallic click.

But soon after I moved in, I began to suspect that the locks were improperly installed. I could never hear that click when I locked the door. I called in a locksmith and it turned out that the hole the workmen had drilled in the door frame was too small. The bolt simply could not penetrate deep enough to lock into place. The locksmith said the door could be opened easily with a screwdriver or even a credit card. I had him install double-cylinder dead bolt locks on both of my doors and calibrate them to open with the same key. There was one key and one spare, and I kept both on my person at all times.

One day, Vama, the woman from Yugoslavia, locked herself out. Shae offered to call management for her but Vama pulled her crocheted shawl tight around her, shaking her head pitifully, so I tried with a credit card. I inserted it between the door and the frame and scraped it hard against the bolt pin. Everyone insisted that it was not possible, but it worked immediately, the bolt popping back, the door slipping open and the stale air rushing out. Shae complained to management about the safety issue implicit in having locks you could open with a credit card, but nobody believed the story.

I considered inviting Vama to the birthday party but almost every time I saw her, she was headed for Yugoslavia. She carried a faded suitcase the blue-gray color of forget-me-nots pressed in an old Sears catalog. A strap ran all the way around the case and the initials VR were embossed on the leather.

Once I saw her at the edge of town. She was walking that faltering walk, tipping all her weight to one foot before moving the other, but moving it inevitably, finding the balance as carefully as if she had been ascending a sheer cliff rather than trudging along the flat strip of River Road where it separated Safeway from the Laundromat. She wore a gray wool coat buttoned all the way up, thick-soled shoes and a round gray hat with a small veil. The coat came well below her knees and a broach was pinned on the lapel. The blue suitcase slowed her progress, but she only set it down to shift it from one hand to the other.

She was headed back to Yugoslavia, she told me in broken English. Back to the old country, to her own people. She would die in the old country, not here among strangers, not with the gas leaks everywhere.

I told her I did not think River Road west would lead her to Yugoslavia, but she swatted away the remark with distaste and, muttering to herself, plodded on past the laundromat and out of town. When I stopped by management, the receptionist rolled her eyes.

"Must be the full moon again," she said. "The poor old thing runs away and there's nobody even to run away from."

I tried to remember the moon the night I came to the river, but memory was not my strong suit. I could only call to mind the blood pounding in my temples, the blurred lights in the rearview mirror as I made my wild escape from my collapsing life. Vama did not get very far. They brought her back later that same evening and she stayed in her cabin and taped newspapers over the windows.

That night I had a dream about Vama. She was lying in

bed, the moonlight shining in the little cabin window. Suddenly the devil appeared in the room, standing erect beside her bedside, his face in shadow. Vama held her breath, certain she would die. The figure towered over her, blocking the moonbeam. She could not see the face, only the huge hands reaching down, the blackness of the shadows. As he bent over her, the ribbon of moonlight appeared again, and she suddenly remembered a trick that she knew, a saving trick that she knew. She shimmered into the air and slipped onto the beam of moonlight. Up, up she traveled, out the window and away, passing straight up to the moon itself, then sliding down another moonbeam to Yugoslavia.

I woke up shivering, skin slippery with sweat. The night pressed in against my window, a thick, black, muffling cloak, and I lay there trembling, struggling to breathe. No line of light slanted into the cabin; and I knew that I was here, alone, forever, without an escape route. I turned on the light beside the bed and kept watch until dawn.

The full moon rose the following day just after sunset when the sky was a clear, hollow pink. It appeared suddenly, whole and huge, the pale bruised face floating just above the treetops like a long-lost friend or enemy. With it came a strange sweet scent that laced the evening breeze, as incense might herald the arrival of someone holy or powerful.

I smelled it again the next morning: the usual hint of earthy bitter green was edged with a hot sweetness. I could not identify it and even as I inhaled, it faded and disappeared. The pit bull, lying vigilant in its customary place in the footpath, lifted its head to smell too. It pulled itself up and edged two or three feet closer to the table, lying down again and going to sleep immediately as though the three feet it had moved were all that was necessary to keep the Brute safe from harm. I went to the cafe, but the coast was not clear there either.

Jack the maintenance man stopped by the cafe that morning. He had no memory whatsoever of closing up my window, but he remembered fixing my sink when it fell off the wall and was very proud of it. He bought a coffee to go and insisted on drinking it at my table.

Jack was going places. He said that first off. He was a musician but had been unemployed before the flood and finally landed this job with the management company. He was inexperienced but handy and, anyway, things were going to change for him pretty quickly because he was ready now. He seemed to meet Shae's criteria, so I invited him to the birthday party.

The cafe had not been willing to put an ocean or a bus on the cake, but they agreed to write "Happy Birthday Larry" in blue letters and draw in a wave or two and to provide one of those candles that will not blow out. They made a mistake on the name and wrote "Harry" instead of "Larry," but the cafe owner fixed it so the "H" hardly showed, and I took it anyway.

When I told Shae about the incident, she paled and sat down and did not say a word for some minutes. Finally, she lit a cigarette and fluffed the sides of her hair. Harry was Larry's psychopath brother, she told me. She should never have mentioned him that morning. She had invited trouble.

Shae and I prepared for the party at four-thirty. There wasn't much to do. She had a package of balloons and we blew up a few and tied them to the willow tree, then sat drinking coffee. The party was to begin at five that afternoon. It was almost six when Jack strolled up the footpath from Fourth Street carrying his guitar. He had just come from a local bar where he had played a few songs and passed the hat. He sat down as close to me as he could get.

Shae did not say anything about the time. She stretched her tongue out, curling it up toward her nose. "So, you plan to play the River?" she asked. "It's a tough market in winter."

"Oh, I don't intend to be here by winter," Jack said, glancing at me and winking. "Things are going to start opening up for me. Things are going to start changing fast."

"I'd better get Larry," Shae said.

Larry was in their cabin watching Columbo. It was a few minutes before Shae led him out. He had sleeked his hair back with water and was wearing a red sweater, the cheery color of a child's Christmas stocking. His skin looked almost blue-white next to it. His eyes were wide and he clutched his tall plastic container of Coke close to his chest like a terrified child. I knew fear when I saw it and was about to call the whole thing off, then suddenly he said hello and his strong, perfect teeth appeared and everything was all right again.

Jack shook Larry's hand and said, "Happy birthday." Then he pushed back his end of the bench to give himself room, strummed a few chords and started to sing. It was a number he had written. I counted eleven verses. The music floated up and over the high wooden fence and Shae and I clapped when he was done. Larry carefully put down his glass of Coke and clapped too.

Jack waited until the applause died away then played another number. It was longer. Halfway through it, Larry got up and disappeared inside the cabin. Jack played a third song before he put the guitar aside. I brought out the cake and the plates. Larry had come back to the table by then. He poured himself a glass of Coke, tipping the liquid slowly as though trying to avoid bubbles but there were no bubbles. It was completely flat.

Jack grabbed for the guitar again but this time he played "Happy Birthday," singing it too, his deep voice filling Garden Court. Shae and I sang along. With the last, long "happy birthday to you," everyone looked expectantly at Larry but we had forgotten to light the candle so there was nothing to blow out. Shae pulled out her Bic lighter, but it would not work so she went off to search for her matches on the deck. She talked as she looked, telling us about her disability hearing and how the hospital had put pressure on her doctor not to testify. She raised her hands dramatically, peering back at the table and shrugging. When she started in on the flood, Larry stood up and retreated into the cabin again.

Shae located the matches and came back to the table. "It's still hard to believe that the water was over the top of my house," she said, shaking her head.

"Where do you live?" Jack asked.

I looked at the door to Shae's cabin. It was some ten

feet from where we were sitting. Larry walked out of it and sat down again. He did not meet my eyes.

"You fixed my wiring a week ago," Shae told Jack.

"Did I?" he said. "It means so little to me, this handy-man stuff. But I won't be doing this for long. Everything's gonna be changing for me, but fast, as *she* knows." He looked at me, lifting his glass. Shae looked at me and rolled her eyes.

I lit the birthday candle and we sang the song again. Larry blew air at the flame, a shallow puff as if he did not have lungs at all, but there was only the one candle and it went out. Everyone clapped and he smiled for the first time and looked around proudly. The flame had completely left the long wick, but a spark of life must have remained hidden somewhere in the thin rope because a few seconds later, the flame popped out again, like a clown from a box at the circus. Larry thought he had not done it right. I told him that it was a trick candle, but he lifted his eyebrows and concentrated terribly on blowing out the little flame. Again, the fire seemed to be completely extinguished; ten seconds later it popped out again from wherever it had been hiding. Larry put his hand over his mouth. Then he reached over, picked off the candle carefully, and stuffed it, tip first, into the blue frosting waves.

It was still light when everyone stood up to go, the cool violet sky scarred by ragged clouds. As I approached the trellis, I saw that the five crucifixes were again tacked to the outside of Felicia's door.

CHAPTER 5

LARRY BEGAN HALLUCINATING sometime after midnight. He started mumbling something about a job he had and his high school principal. Shae let it go on for a while, then she came over to tell me.

"Here I go again," she said. "They say he does it to be like his dad. I mean come on! His father didn't mean to kill himself; he was trying to shoot Larry."

Shae peered into the cabin as I put on shoes. She twisted her head toward the kitchen, perhaps looking for family photos on the refrigerator but its white face was blank. I had the photos buried deep in boxes, my dad standing tall, my mom's slight smile, my sister's trusting eyes. They say a stable childhood creates stable adults, but it does not always work as planned. I was living proof, the distorted bud on the perfect shrub.

I followed Shae out into the night. Beyond the dark expanse of the deck, a yellow light illuminated the front of her cabin. The light seeped down in particles through the thick air, pooling just outside the cabin door. Shae reached through the yellow haze to grasp the doorknob. She pushed the door open and stood outside with her arm extended the width of it.

Larry's thin body lay jumbled across the mattress on the floor as if flung there by some careless or violent hand. He was still wearing the red birthday sweater. He lay on his back, his head turned toward the wall. His legs, bent at odd angles, spilled off the mattress onto the green-gray rug like a painting I had seen of a man cut loose on a raft at sea. Ashes swirled from the tipped ashtray onto the rug and the cigarette smell washed toward the door.

I blocked the rising panic so completely that I could have been Columbo, walking in calmly, scanning the body for signs of life. Larry wasn't dead. The chest moved slightly, up and down. My first instinct was to look for blood but of course there was no blood. I touched the neck; the pulse beat a slow rhythm. I called his name once, twice, and then shook the shoulder. It moved easily enough but fell back when I let it go.

Shae hadn't called the emergency number yet, so I did it. When someone answered, I told them about Larry. But when they asked if he had taken anything, I had to pass the receiver to Shae. She was standing outside the cabin smoking. She sucked greedily on the cigarette and reached for the phone.

"Mellaril, Elavil and Valium," she said into the receiver. "His shrink prescribes them in quart bottles. Can you believe it? That many meds, and for an addict. They're death for addicts as he knows, that shrink. I know he knows it because I told him myself."

She inhaled more smoke from the cigarette, leaning back against the outside wall of the cabin for support. The yellow light soiled the front of her body.

"An alcoholic, an addict," she continued. "I mean, hello there, you don't give a six-month supply of anti-psychotic meds to an addict without asking for a lawsuit."

Across the room, Larry moaned suddenly and said something about a job after school. I hurried back to the mattress and took the pulse again. It seemed weaker. I counted, thirty seconds, forty beats. Shae kept talking and I counted off another forty heartbeats. It was a hard fact, something to hold onto. I planned to tell the emergency people the pulse and moved toward the door, but by the time I got there, Shae had already hung up.

"Larry's just so trusting," Shae said to me, as if we had been speaking the whole time. "He thinks the shrink's a doctor so he must know. Doctors, ha! Look at that shrink that testified in Harry's rape trial. He does hours of testing to establish that Harry's a violent psychopath, then admits in open court that there's no difference in the psychological makeup of a rapist and a normal man." She crushed out her cigarette stub fiercely, as if the gesture could destroy Larry's enemies and her own.

"Then my own doctor on this disability claim," she continued. "He better not sell me out, he had just better not." She began to talk about the hearing, how they had been ready to settle up because it was obvious she could not bend over a keyboard with a neck in the condition of hers, and all she wanted was rehab, training to be a paralegal. Then they got to her doctor. She was not about to sit still for a cover-up. Rehab would not settle the matter if there were a cover-up. She pressed her lips together and her eyes narrowed into slits. In the case of a cover-up, she would insist on a cash settlement.

While she talked, my eyes moved from Larry's body to my watch and back again, my ears strained for the wail of an ambulance. The body did not move. Was Larry dead? I was bracing myself to check the pulse again when a light appeared up the footpath, then shadowy figures like clumps of darkness independent from the rest of the night.

"George and Robbie, his fishing friends," she told me. "They planned an early start."

The figures approached quickly, materializing out of the thick dark. A man was in the lead, a young man with an athletic body and a freckled face. He wore a cap with fishing flies stuck into it and carried a flashlight. The girl, Robbie, came after. She smiled and waved.

"Forget the fishing," Shae told them. "Larry's OD-ed on those meds again. We're waiting for the ambulance."

George pushed past Shae to the door of the cabin. He stepped into the cabin, around the overturned ashtray, the two-liter coke bottle, several coffee mugs. It seemed there were hundreds of things on the floor. George bent down and seized Larry's shoulder, shaking it roughly. When he released it, the shoulder fell back. George stood up, breathed out long through his nose. Then he took off the fishing cap and threw it as hard as he could against the far wall of the cabin. I turned and walked out of the cabin.

Robbie was on the deck with Shae, talking quietly. They were almost the same height, but Robbie stood between

Shae and the cabin light, covering Shae with shadow. "What could have happened?" she asked softly. I leaned closer to hear as if the answer were terribly important, as if it could solve all the burning questions in my own life.

Shae's cigarette had gathered a long ash. It fell as she raised the cigarette to her mouth, fell and hit the deck, exploding soundlessly. Her face collapsed into her chin. "He just wanted to be like everyone else," she said. "That's all he's ever wanted, to be like everyone else."

George walked out of Shae's cabin, his body stiff. He shook his head grimly, smacking his flashlight into his left palm, over and over.

"Let's get him out of here," he said.

"The ambulance . . ." I said.

"Last time it took an hour to get here," he said. "The River's not high on the priority list."

Shae hustled out to bring her car around and the rest of us went back into the cabin. George stood at the head of the mattress. He seized Larry's arms under the shoulders and Robbie ran around to move things out of the way while I found the feet, red socks, old high-top tennis shoes. The legs were light until the torso connected. We backed the body down the stairs, bumping several times, then set it down in the footpath. Nobody came out from any of the cabins.

Larry groaned. He muttered something under his breath. The light from my cabin fell on his face. It looked crushed in, his face, as though someone had said "close your eyes and open your mouth," then hit him just below the nose with a brick.

"Larry!" George yelled. "Larry, god-damn you." There was no answer and even the muttering stopped. We tried to lift him again, but the arms and legs were no longer dead weight. Each headed in a different direction, still limp but writhing as if stiff metal ribbons flexed inside instead of bones. It was impossible to carry him.

George said to put the body down. When it was on the ground, he shoved up the top of the torso until the head and shoulders leaned over the legs, sitting the body up there on the footpath. He wrapped his arms around it from the back, his own hands joining on the chest. He gave a tug and vomit flowed out of the mouth, down the beard, the red sweater. The head hung forward, loose on the spiny neck. George cursed, then tried again. In the end, we each grabbed an arm and dragged it down the footpath to Shae's car.

I walked back into Garden Court alone. The deck was now in darkness. Only my own cabin blazed with light, the sharp bright edges against the soft night making the cabin seem completely empty, hollowed out like a Jack-o'-lantern. I flipped the switch from the doorway, then sat down on the stairs to the deck. The night was thick, heavy as it is with clouds, but there were no clouds. The stars pierced the dark like pinholes, twinkling coldly, far away.

As my eyes adjusted, I could still make out the courtyard. The little pit bull was not there. Across the footpath was my cabin, then the picnic table, then Michael's cabin. Garden Court was the same at night as it was during the day except that the circle of vision ended at the fence. It was as if the courtyard existed alone, unconnected to any street, any city, suspended all by itself in the universe. It looked strange suddenly, unreal, and I got that weird feeling like I was watching it on television. I looked around carefully. Vampires and ghosts and werewolves are supposed to come out at night, but I could not see any, only my own reflection in my cabin window, just the pale face, the bulk of the body blending in with the dark.

I noticed the cold on my arm, the fact of it, like looking at a color and knowing it is blue. I knew it was cold, my arm, then I went to the other arm and it was cold too. The little hairs stood up like icicles forming swords outside the eaves of a house in a cold climate when it warms just a little; long frozen tubes of water, drip, drip, dripping in the spring like faucets. They could kill you if they broke off because they fell with great weight, picking up speed toward the ground. A girl was killed once by an icicle falling off the roof of a tunnel and piercing her heart.

Larry's heart had still been beating when we put him in the back of Shae's wagon. I remembered his chest moving slightly, up, down, almost against his will. You could not kill yourself by deciding to stop breathing. You could hold your breath but once you passed out your body started breathing again. In the chain of death, the body was the weakest link, the weakest link of all.

I began to sweat, then my teeth started chattering crazily and everything seemed to move farther and farther away. I tried to hold on by focusing on the bushes in front of the deck cabins. There were five bushes, five in a row. The one nearest the alley was slightly taller than the rest.

I leaned over and touched a cold, flat leaf. I wondered if plants stop breathing when they find themselves in danger but of course plants do not breathe the same way animals do and they never harm themselves.

Animals do not stop breathing when faced with danger. They turn to defend themselves or run if they are small. But what if they cannot run? A skunk caught in the headlight beams probably knocks itself out, even though it does not fall over, it sends itself to somewhere safe, to a favorite tree, a green meadow, where it is just autumn and the sky is smoky and cold with clouds and light puffs of wind dip the tops of the blue bells and the skunk runs across the meadow toward its tree and is sitting close to its thick, fragrant bark by the time the rubber hits and flattens the black fur into a little strip of asphalt with a white line down the middle.

CHAPTER 6

I AROSE EARLY AND headed to the cafe the next morning, as usual. The dawn was smudgy, cold, as it is after a storm. Shae's cabin seemed a small thing, frail and haphazard, an item of flotsam left grounded in the wake of the previous night. The blinds were pulled down tight and I could not detect any signs of life.

As I left Garden Court, my eyes searched the footpath for evidence of the crime, but of course there was no evidence since there had been no crime. No crime, no blood, no screams in the night. Instead, the footpath appeared strangely immaculate, brushed and tidied by the sweep of Larry's body against it.

I bought my coffee, sat at my usual table, my shoulders aching, hard as stone. I flipped through the newspaper, but there was nothing about Larry or Garden Court. It was as if nothing had happened. Somehow, I was always the only witness to crimes that had not occurred. What would Columbo make of that?

The big news event was Clean-Up Week, organized by

local merchants to put a good face on the public areas of the town before the summer season. Residents were asked to participate in scheduled clean-up activities, like picking up garbage from the river beach and repainting the library. All week, trucks would pass to haul away bulky garbage. There was to be a fair afterward with a free barbeque.

However, the clean-up campaign had its opposition, people who seemed to view the clean-up as a whitewash of blame. Every time a clean-up sign or banner appeared, it was altered with a marker or paint to read "cover-up." From my seat in the cafe, I could see the banner suspended across River Road. They had strung it up only yesterday, but it was already altered to read "Cover-Up Week." Even the bumper stickers the Chamber of Commerce distributed were amended to read "We Support the Cover-Up."

The newspaper said that the protest was related to the general speculation that the flood damage was not caused by an act of God, but by the big city up-river deliberately opening its own flood gates and dooming the little town. The paper had a Reporter-on-the-Street column with photos of residents above their opinions on the Clean-Up Week question. I recognized a photo of the middle-aged veteran who lived in Garden Court with his mother. Her photo was there too. Each of them supported the clean-up efforts but believed the deeper damage to the wooden structures was beyond repair.

I did not know any of the other people polled. A woman with her hair braided on both sides said that the flood was over and it was time for everyone to put it behind them. Another woman believed that the question of blame was not relevant; the town had to spiff itself up if it wanted to attract tourists. "Nobody likes a crying child," she said.

Two other residents were questioned, both of them men. One agreed with the women and one did not. The newspaper had accidentally repeated the same photo above both of these opinions, a photo of a man with small features and some scar or mark slicing his right cheek.

I walked back down Fourth Street through the warm sunlight of late morning, past car after car bearing the altered bumper stickers: *We support the cover-up.* Every time I saw one, light little wings fluttered in my heart, a mounting and inexplicable defiance.

Back in Garden Court, Shae's cabin remained dark and silent. When I turned to my own cabin, there was something spilled over my front stairs. It was dark and wet. My heart started hammering immediately, even before my mind realized that it was blood, my front steps were slick with blood. Blood was spattered around my doormat and up the path. My head started spinning and I braced a hand against the cabin wall to keep from falling.

While I stood staring at the cabin stairs, the cooking lady from the Fourth Street cabin marched down the footpath carrying a sack of garbage. Her large face was pale with horizontal lines on her forehead but her back was very straight. She told me that a big black dog had jumped the pit right in front of Garden Court an hour back, fighting into the street, a devil dog with a huge head and wide chest. Her kids saw it and called to her. The black dog did not snarl or growl; it just clamped its teeth on the little pit's leg and blood started pouring everywhere, but the pit twisted out of the grip. It was holding its own when the veteran came out and fired a pistol and the black dog took off. The little pit ran back into Garden Court and sat on that doorstep shivering and bleeding like a faucet. Her kids were scared, she said, so she took her broom and shooed it away, off to the woods to die. She was not hard-hearted, she told me, but she had her children to think of.

The veteran emerged from his cabin. It was almost as if he had been standing behind his own door listening. He was tall and stocky, muscular, with a thick neck and enormous hands.

"There was no reason to run him off," the veteran said. His voice was soft, but it carried peculiarly well.

"You'd run off a rabid dog if you had children," the cooking lady told him. "They're a lot of trouble but they're my own flesh and blood," she said. "Flesh of my flesh, bone of my bone."

This seemed a good time to leave and I moved toward my cabin door. No dogs, I reminded myself. Certainly, no rabid dogs.

"That dog's not rabid," the veteran said. He leaned against the railing on the deck and spoke without looking at the cooking lady. He did not look at me either as I unlocked my cabin door. He seemed to be looking past the weeping willow at something we could not see.

"That dog's not rabid," he repeated. "He's heartbroken."

I stopped, key in the door. I heard the wind whispering in the weeping willow, cries of children playing from the street. A car rattled by on Fourth. I turned back toward him.

"Heartbroken?" I said. The word hung small in the big air.

"He used to have people," the veteran said. "People, his people. When they dumped him here after the flood, pretty much broke his heart. He keeps waiting for them to come back and get him but they're not coming back."

"I'd keep him myself," the veteran continued, "but you can't trust him now; once a dog's had his heart broken, you can never trust him again."

The veteran went back into his cabin and the cooking lady continued to the garbage cans. I stood silently on the doorstep for a few minutes while little disconnected pieces of sorrow drifted slowly toward the earth like snowflakes through lamplight. The only safe course was to proceed into my cabin. But I couldn't. I relocked my door and walked out of Garden Court to Fourth Street.

Up toward the cafe, past the Bordeaux Vet Clinic, men worked on a pickup truck in the street. The diesel storage yard was on the right, the sooty tanks crowded along the inside boundary of the lot, and a black Doberman slept near the fence at the back of the flat, dirty yard. On the opposite side of the street was a grassy lot littered with bottles. The little pit bull was not there.

I crossed the lot and the dirt alley and walked into the park. The tramps' beer cans stood neatly in the garbage can beneath the gnarled tree. The field was empty. I started back toward the woods.

The wooded section of the park began suddenly as if there were a boundary line which the redwoods would not cross. The trees lined up thick and deep behind that border.

A narrow path passed through the dim quiet and the trees stood back from it, shadowing it from above. There was not much undergrowth, only the redwoods and the low clover leaves of redwood sorrel. The path was padded with dead leaves and redwood needles that exploded in soft cracks as I took each step.

I walked for some time. The path widened and the terrain sloped up, gradually at first then suddenly steeply. It was dark and cold and quiet except for the snapping of the leaf-spines under my feet. It felt familiar, that path, as if I had walked it before, walked this very same path before in search of something, and certain images leaped out at me as if I already knew them: a fallen redwood that had been caught by another before it hit the ground; the arrangement of three broad stones inside the burned-out center of a husky trunk; the slant of filtered sunlight where the path turned sharply. Still, I kept moving, inhaling the loamy forest smell and listening carefully to the padding and cracking of my feet against the earth.

Eventually the hill crested. The path turned sharply to the right and narrowed, heading down. Just there, on the left, a figure loomed, a dark figure some ten feet back from the path, wrapped in shadow. It was a statue - life-size maybe taller - positioned on a rock base. The figure was of dark wood, carved with flowing robes and a hood shrouding the face. It held a cross in front of it, the crossbeams long and of equal length like a tire iron, the halo a round disk on the statue's head like a full moon rising directly behind it. It was not clear what Christian figure it was supposed to represent. The face was small and triangular, floating too deep in the wooden folds of the hood to distinguish father from son, master from disciple. The features were rough, the eyes horizontal slits very close together, the mouth high and straight and thin under a thin nose. The cheekbones gouged sharply back to nothing.

A few hundred yards beyond the statue, the path descended, then opened suddenly into brilliant sunlight. I walked to the edge of that sunlight and looked down into a wide, sloping clearing. A small amphitheater had been built there sometime long ago, with benches made of rock and wood placed in descending, semi-circle rows. Some of the benches lay fallen in the dirt. In the front was a kind of altar, a round raised platform some twenty feet across with a railing around it.

Again, I felt the familiarity, like I had seen it all before, seen it all from just that angle, knew the horror that had happened here. All my answers were here, I knew it. I walked down the aisle, past the fallen benches. There was no sound in the whole world but my own breathing, loud as the ocean, in, out, like waves. I stopped my breath and stood still a few moments beside the altar, hands trembling slightly, and then I forced my eyes to look over. The altar was the stump of a giant redwood tree. The dog's body was not there. Nothing was there but a scattering of empty bottles.

When I got back to Garden Court, everything was quiet. I opened my cabin to air it out and spent the afternoon working in the garden. The dark earth seemed cool and real and the rhythm of digging slowed everything down inside me, but, still, I kept an eye out for the pit bull. I reminded myself that I was not involved here, but if the dog were alive, I would help it find a home. It would go no further than that.

Mid-afternoon, I heard a bolt lock pushed back. Michael eased open his door and peered around the picnic area. He saw that I saw him, so he stepped all the way out of the door as if he had intended to survey the day.

"How is he?" Michael asked.

I said that I had not been able to find him, that he had taken off and nobody had seen him."He took off?" Michael repeated. "On his own? Where would he go?"

I repeated what the cooking woman had told me, that he had gone off to the woods to die. Michael stared at me. He did not withdraw his gaze into himself as usual, but he stood, rooted to the spot, and stared at me.

"They said his ears were all bloody," I said.

"Jesus," Michael said. He closed his cabin door slowly and walked haltingly over to the table as if drawn there against his will.

"How did he get out?" Michael said.

I looked up. "Get out?"

"Didn't Shae get him to the hospital?"

Something snapped inside me then, I felt it crack like a sheet of glass. Laughter rose inside me. I leaned hard over the table to stop it, but it rose like a flood inside me and though I clenched my stomach and bit the inside of my cheek, laughter sniffed out through my nose.

Michael retreated a few steps, staring hard at me.

"The dog," I managed to explain.

Michael's eyes softened a little, but he kept his distance.

"The dog ran off," I said. "Not Larry." I thought of Larry escaping to the woods, his skinny legs pumping below the hospital gown, Larry, leaping over fallen redwood branches. It wasn't funny and I leaned over the table trying not to laugh but laughing silently, until my stomach ached like from gagging. I had not laughed in a long time and it felt I should say an act of contrition, but the boy was laughing too.

"I wondered how his ears got bloody," Michael said.

"Whose ears were bloody?" Shae asked, appearing on the deck in front of her cabin. I laughed more and Michael leaned against the wall of his cabin, his face wide open, and laughed and laughed. Shae scowled slightly but waited it out. When I was able to explain, she gave a laugh too.

"Hah!" she declared. "Larry can't sit up in bed, let alone get up and run off. He'll be in ICU for a week." The laughter passed completely and you could hear the shuffling of willow leaves.

"Now, where's that dog?" she demanded. "I found someone in the Program who might take it."

"If the Brute comes back," Michael said.

"He'll come back," Shae assured him. "It's never the stray dogs that die."

The Brute slunk back into Garden Court the next evening as a breeze stirred up the air. He was alive. I leaped to my feet and shouted out "He's back!" and Michael appeared at his door. The dog walked toward us then slowed, looked around, and finally stopped in its customary place in the footpath. At first it did not look very different, still wary, still completely alone, but when I got closer, I saw that its ear was ripped, and one front leg was caked with dried blood. I put some tuna fish on a plate and the dog edged over and ate it down.

"Shae's got a home for you old Brute," Michael told him.

"Maybe," Shae called out from her cabin. "No promises."

"The Brute needs a real name," Michael said. "Nobody will take a dog without a real name." No one responded to this suggestion, but that did not seem to bother Michael.

"You sure are ugly, Brute," Michael said to the dog. It came over and sat next to his legs, but its wide eyes looked at me. The wind ceased and the leaves hung limp, listening.

A name came into my head. "Brutus," I said, before I could stop myself.

Michael peered down at the dog. "Maybe Brutus," he allowed. He inspected the thin, muddy back carefully. "Hi there Brutus," he said. He reached down cautiously and patted the dog's triangular skull with two fingers.

I knew in that instant that everything that happened after would be my own fault.

The next day was even warmer. Spring was in full swing, the days losing their memory of winter. Shae's friends were coming in the afternoon to take a look at the dog, so I decided to wash it off. I screwed the hose into the tap in the front of my cabin. The water spit a few times before it flowed out in a thick stream. I positioned myself in the sun near the deck, then called the dog over and sprayed its back. It ran fast up the footpath.

Michael came out. "Brutus doesn't like the hose," he said.

"Hold him still," I said.

"Not me," Michael shook his head.

I shrugged and turned to spray the willow instead. I put both hands around the trigger of the nozzle and pressed it all the way down; the water sprayed out fast and hard. I tilted it up so that it arced across the footpath to the tree.

The dog stopped in his tracks and turned. It started running back up the footpath toward me. It picked up speed as it approached, then it lunged toward me and leaped, and I jumped back and heard the dog's teeth clip together in the air. It landed ten feet down the footpath.

Michael was on his feet. "Look out!" he yelled. "He's after the water!"

The dog stood alert, tail wagging, eyes on the nozzle. I recovered my balance then stepped back to where I had been. I pushed down the trigger again and shot the tight line of water into the air across the footpath. The dog rushed it again, leaping and turning mid-air to try to get at the spray as if it were something solid.

Whenever I moved the hose slightly, the dog jumped again, his teeth snapping together around the tube of water, seeking some solid core but meeting only themselves. Michael clapped his hands and laughed. When I turned off the hose, the dog shook himself from head to toe, then wagged his tail.

"He's clean now," Michael said, and it was true. The dog's white markings were no longer muddy. His main color was a gold-brown brindle, but his paws looked as if he had waded into a tub of white paint. His face was splashed with white, too, like a Hereford cow. A third color, black, ran along his back and around the prominent ribs, but much of the hair was missing on his rump and what remained grew in mangy clumps among the sores and scars.

Shae's friends arrived in the afternoon, a man and a woman walking up the footpath. The woman was tall, over six feet, big and healthy looking. Although the man walked in front of her, keeping his body smack between Shae and the woman, I could see the woman perfectly, her plump-cheeked, placid face, her hair cut into high bangs with the rest caught behind in a messy ponytail. Her arms were thick but firm without being muscled at all, like huge baby arms.

The man looked familiar, but I could not place him. He was wiry, muscular, with a forward curve to the upper body and head, and his arms hanging loose, slightly forward, ready. He gave me the once-over, and then turned to the dog. I stood back, letting him have all the room he needed, but the man objected to the dog immediately.

"I thought you said it was pit," he said to Shae, scowling.

"It's a pit," Shae said. "Look at the neck." The dog had a pretty thick neck and wide shoulders. It looked at the couple warily. The man frowned and the woman towered behind him, her big moon face expressionless.

"This is no guard dog," he said. "I need a guard dog back there at my place."

"At Tina's place?" Shae asked. The man stiffened up

straight, except for the slight forward hulk to his upper body. Something about the stance was menacing, familiar.

"Our place," he said. "A real pit would keep people away."

"You don't like company anymore Tina?" Shae asked. The woman smiled just perceptibly, as though it were an inside joke between her and Shae, but the mouth movement came and went before the man's glance hit her, so he did not say anything.

Shae stretched out her tongue, curling it up in that gesture. "His name is Brutus," she said.

"Brutus," the man repeated appreciatively. He snapped his fingers. "Come here Brutus." The dog stood up and moved slightly farther away. When the man walked toward him, he bared his teeth without making a sound.

"What's wrong with its teeth?" the man asked. The left side of the dog's muzzle was directly in view, but I couldn't see anything unusual.

"It's a definite no if someone's filed his teeth down," the man said. "Don't want a dog someone else has broken."

Shae said the dog was malnourished and maybe regular calcium would take care of it, but the man snorted. He lifted his forehead at the woman. She produced a pack of cigarettes from her purse and handed it to him. He lit one, sucked in, then hard at the dog for some minutes before he shook his head.

"Nope," he said with great finality and I let out my breath. I realized that I had been holding my breath for a long, long time.

As they were walking away, Shae called out to Tina,

"See you at the meeting tonight?" The big face smiled but no answer came back. Shae sat down at the picnic table and Michael emerged again from his cabin. He sat on his steps.

"Brutus," he called, and the dog ran to him. "Well Brutus, you blew that one," Michael told him. "Look, there's nothing wrong with his teeth."

"What a jerk," Shae hissed. "You don't have to be white trash to live on the river, but it helps. Tina's a sweet girl but," she lowered her voice, "goes in and out of the Program like you wouldn't believe."

"Are you in AA?" Michael asked me.

I shook my head.

"Me neither," Michael said. "I can quit whenever I want."

"Only you never want," Shae said, nodding her head with her lips pressed together in a sort of smile. "Uh-huh. I used to say that too."

"I can," Michael said. "I quit for four months last year when my brother was back."

"Lots of alkies go dry for a few months," Shae told him. "Then they always start back up. To really quit, you have to work the Program. You have to go to meetings."

"Larry doesn't," Michael said.

"Yeah, and look what happened to him," she said. "Another dash to St. Joe's Emergency in the middle of the night. But the OD wasn't all his fault. That shrink's giving him those meds in laundry-baskets. I mean, hello there, you don't give that many meds to an addict without asking for a lawsuit. Hah! At least now he'll have to stop."

Larry came back from the hospital a week later. I saw him walking slowly up the footpath, but I did not see him again for two days. He stayed inside their cabin and I did not go over. The third day was clear and warm. I was outside, watering the bushes in front of the deck. Michael sat on his front steps, eating cookies and feeding Brutus some bits.

Larry walked out the door of his cabin onto the deck. I saw him out of the corner of my eye, but I kept hosing, thinking of what to say. Finally I released the trigger of the nozzle and prepared to turn around and say "Larry, good to see you," when Michael saw him and said, "Larry, you're back."

"Yup," Larry said. He stood carefully at the deck railing, carrying his emaciated body cautiously as if his bones were not connected at all but held together only by balance. The one-eyed cat lay on the railing and Larry rubbed its head with a finger and did not look up. In the long silence, I could almost hear the sound of his finger against the fur.

"Show him Brutus with the water," Michael said, taking another bite of cookie.

"Brutus?" Larry said. He was not wearing his teeth and he slurred the "s."

"Brutus," Michael affirmed between chews. "She named him."

I turned on the hose again and pressed the trigger down hard, arching the stream high across the footpath. The water gleamed silver-gray in the sunlight, curving like a sword seven or eight feet above the dusty earth. The dog was on his feet and running, before I looked around, running, building speed, then leaping high, turning his body into the arch; at the top of the leap he seemed to pause, pure muscle and action suspended, then his teeth sank into the stream at its highest point and he was back on the ground shaking himself.

Larry's shriveled face opened up in an incredulous smile.

"Oh boy," he said. "Will he do it again?"

CHAPTER 7

THE DAY DAWNED like any other, up early in the cool morning, the brisk walk to the cafe. From my seat near the window, I watched the town arrange its summer face. Boarded-up store fronts opened into bright boutiques selling kites or pottery or sand toys. It was cheerful but hollow, the summer face, with the deep, empty energy of someone who spends the day in bed in gray despair, then puts on a bright smile for callers. The summer face was like that, smiling broadly and putting on coffee, and it left a faint nausea. But mornings, early, you could still catch the winter face looking up at you from dirty bed sheets, eyes full of fear or nothing.

After the cafe that morning I traced the same path back, past the vet clinic, the mental health center. I saw old Michael on Fourth Street, lecturing the rough-looking homeless man called Bear about his hygiene. But Michael winked at me as I passed and I saw nothing disturbing.

It was when I began my gardening chores that I first noticed something amiss: pale oval pods in the bushes in front of the deck cabins, whitish balls clustered on the base of the leaves. Mealy bugs. I recognized them immediately from the Safeway book, soft-bodied insects that attack the new growth of a plant. The book said to react quickly, that mealy bugs sucked the life out of young plants. The cartoon illustration showed a scared little plant trapped in its pot with big bugs approaching, so I hurried to the hardware store and bought powdered pesticide and a pump sprayer.

Back in Garden Court, I measured the large-grain powder into the belly of the metal sprayer. I added water and shook the sprayer back and forth releasing the active ingredients until I tasted the poison on my tongue, queer synthetic fumes like burning plastic. I carried a chair from my cabin out onto the deck and I climbed up with the sprayer. But when I leaned over the first bush, I saw that the oval pods were not mealy bugs. They were not bugs at all. They were flower buds. There were white buds on every branch.

In just a few days, the bushes in front of the deck cabins overflowed with flowers. Flowers rushed to open, wave after wave of them, white and pink and mauve. Shae identified them immediately as azalea and the veteran's mother called them hybrid rhododendron, and in a week the thinner branches dipped toward earth with their load of blossoms. Bees came out of nowhere to sip the nectar, and, later, the flash of tiny hummingbirds. Overnight the deck became occupied territory, and when I watered the bushes early in the morning, flowers bobbed heads to greet me in a language I knew but could not remember, as if familiar faces I could not place came calling at the door.

Maybe it had begun earlier but I had not seen it; I had not seen it. Suddenly I saw bright new growth tipping the branches of the redwoods. Suddenly I noticed buds swelling along the thin arms of every shrub and bush. Even the desolate trellis vine blazed green around the base, then began the slow climb, small needy fingers finding easy handholds in last year's dead growth.

"God's in his heaven, all's right with the world," Michael's mother said to Shae one Tuesday as she carried grocery bags up the path. A slight breeze ruffled her hair and she looked softer, like maybe summer had touched her too. But Shae said, "Well, where the hell's he been all these years?"

It felt wrong at first, and then right, painfully, unexpectedly right: new smells, new colors, warm rays of sun poking into the darkest corners calling creatures out of hiding. Quick brown-striped lizards darted up and down the pillars supporting the deck, pausing on the sunlit patio to soak up warmth. Dragonflies and butterflies blew by, batteries of ants stormed the kitchen door.

One morning Michael brought his lunch to the picnic table. He only had a sandwich, but he carried it out cautiously on a yellow plate with a design of the planets around the rim. He also brought out a linen napkin and a knife and fork and spoon. Michael arranged these items on the table carefully, ceremoniously, like a priest organizing the chalice, then, using knife and fork, he cut the crust from each slice of bread until not a single, darkened edge remained. He ate the remaining white square with his fingers. The pit bull sat nearby. When Michael finished his meal, he offered the dog a small piece of crust, and then another, one by one. After that, he sat there with the dog and they both watched me garden. From then on, Michael brought his lunch out every day.

Shae and Larry would appear sometime before noon. Shae was generally rushing off to an AA meeting or on an errand, but Larry would sit in the sun with his family-sized coke bottle and smoke a cigarette and drink a glass of coke companionably without saying much. Once he asked whether I'd received any response to my notice about Brutus in the lost-and-found column of the paper. When I shook my head, he patted the dog and said cheerfully: "Well Big B, nobody wants you."

"Somebody wants him," Michael interjected. "The dogcatcher." Both of them laughed at this. Then Michael brought out a checkerboard and asked Larry to play and they kept it up for hours. Michael loved to win and Larry didn't mind losing so it worked out well.

A few days later, the dogcatcher returned to Garden Court. He strutted in under the trellis, short and muscular and dressed like a policeman with the name of the pound on the badge he wore. His face was grim, with small eyes and thin lips. He spotted the dog right away, lying by the picnic table where Michael was finishing his lunch. The dog did not run away this time, but Michael's face drained of blood and he rose to his feet and backed silently into his cabin, one furtive step at a time. Larry, standing on the deck, moved closer to his own cabin door. I took fast, shallow breaths, little jolts of electricity running up and down my arms.

The pit bull sat alone by the table. It stood up warily watching the man approach. In my mind, I urged the dog to bolt through the hole in the fence like he had the other times, but Brutus held his ground as the man drew closer. My hands began to tremble, and I told myself to stay out of it. This type of situation could trigger an episode, like with Larry and many other times before. But the dog was so small, his head on the level of the man's knees, and sunlight slanted warm into the clearing. I found myself stepping over, asking if there was a problem. The dogcatcher lit a cigarette, holding it with his thumb tip under it and three fingertips above, and said that he'd received complaints about the pit that spring and that he had orders to take it away.

I hid my trembling hands, linking the fingers together behind my back, then pulled out my calm, legal voice. I explained that the dog had lost its owners during the flood, that we'd placed an advertisement to locate the owners and hoped to reunite the dog with them soon, that this would save the pound the trouble of finding a home for it.

The man squinted at me narrowly as if I were crazy and said that any fool could see that the dog was ugly and dangerous. It clearly had been fought and just as clearly had been dumped. He said that the pound never adopted out pit bulls, put them down humanely to discourage organized dog fighting, then sold the dog carcasses to fertilizer companies. A picture flashed before my eye of the dog's body limp in a dark corner, dead eyes staring at nothing, but just as the man finished talking, the little dog jumped to its feet. In one motion, it slid through the hole in the fence into the Mexicans' yard and was gone. I expected the dogcatcher to be furious and could almost see the big hand whip out but instead he laughed because it looked like the dog had been listening and did not want to end up as fertilizer. He smoked that cigarette a little more and said the dog got one more chance after all. He told me to make sure the pound didn't get more complaints about it, maybe pop for a cheap collar so that the pit looked like it belonged to someone.

After the man left, Larry walked over and offered ideas on what color collar to get. Shae came back and heard the story and made instant coffee for all of us. By the time the dog crept back under the fence and Michael edged out to pat it, my hands had stopped shaking and nothing more happened, no further symptoms, a victory. I dished out some of the dog food I'd bought at Safeway and Brutus ate up everything, then fell asleep in a spot of sunlight with his muzzle on Michael's foot.

CHAPTER 8

MICHAEL HAD LITTLE faith in my gardening ability, especially after the mealy bug incident. He told me that management was likely to take the job away from me when they found out how little I knew. But nobody came, and somehow, the garden thrived.

One afternoon Michael opened his door to survey the day and found me turning up soil near his house. "You have dirt all over your face," he commented. "What are you going to plant?"

I handed him the seed packets, sunflowers and blue forget-me-nots.

"Okay," he said, as if his approval were required. "They say 'easy to grow.'"

They were easy to grow. Before long, little shoots emerged from the sunflower seeds. Michael chose a favorite with which he associated his fate, and he pumped a fist in the air and whooped aloud when his sprout grew taller than the others. Maybe his encouragement helped it, because it remained the tallest, day after day, and also produced the first bud. Meanwhile, the low leaves of the forget-me-nots spread across the black earth and, in time, the buds appeared, then opened into blossoms.

"How could they grow so well when you don't know anything about it?" Michael asked. I had no answer, only that I had little to do with their spectacular performance, that they thrived despite my help. It was a kind of magic beyond my explanation, as if I'd stumbled upon a magic wand dropped long ago by some great magician and, waving it about, made a rabbit appear by accident.

One day the veteran's mother came over as I was watering. She was a small, silvery lady with delicate skin and a finely lined face. Her eyes shone a clear blue, like a sky that had never seen rain, but they watered continually, and she kept dabbing them with a Kleenex. That day she was clutching a plant she'd won in a promotional contest at the hardware store, a white rose, she told me proudly. She loved white roses, she said, and wanted someone to plant the bush who really knew what to do. Michael choked on his sandwich laughing but she did not seem to notice.

I read the label aloud, hoping for directions on how to proceed, but it only said that red roses stood for love, pink roses for joy, and white roses for remembrance, so I dug a hole in the soil near her cabin and tucked the plant's roots into it. It was enough. New growth appeared within a week. The veteran's mother checked it regularly, clucking over the new buds and singing them a little French song about *les jolies roses blanches*.

One day, the veteran and his mother were preparing to go to his appointment at the Mental Health Clinic. He sat on a bench on the deck in the late morning sunshine, perfectly still, fixed in time and place like a vehicle with a broken axis, while she hobbled down the two wooden steps to see whether the largest rose bud had opened. She was singing softly about the *jolies roses blanches* and the veteran kneaded his eyes with a calloused hand. But then the song stopped. I looked over. She stood very straight, staring at the rose bud. It had opened in the night. The petals were a buttery yellow.

"It's yellow," she said finally. "It's supposed to be white. White is for remembrance."

The veteran did not look at the rose. He had stopped rubbing his eyes and was staring up at the slow, sad shrug of the weeping willow leaves in the slight breeze. "All the better it's yellow," he told her. "I got remembrance enough for a lifetime."

Shae had seen the veteran have a flashback. It was during the flood, she said, when the police went door to door telling people to leave. The water was already up to her knees and she had Larry moving her things up to high shelves when the cops arrived in Garden Court. One cop pounded on doors getting people moving. Another bellowed through a megaphone: "Okay folks, mandatory evacuation, everybody out, you got ten minutes."

The rain was streaming down in unbroken lines like a shower, and the night was close, pressing in around them. The water lapped into the top of Shae's rubber boots, liquid ice against her freezing feet. Suddenly the electricity went off and the world disappeared, and the police flashlight beams stood out like safety lines in dark water. It felt like a nightmare, scary and unreal at the same time and people were swept out of their cabins and into the night. Emergency personnel pushed through to whisk Vama and Grover out to the waiting bus, carrying the old man in a chair made of their arms. The veteran heard the ruckus, saw the floodlights, even before anyone reached his cabin. He stormed out with his pistol, held the cops at bay, then swarmed over the fence and away.

"He panicked," Shae told me. "His eyes were crazy. I thought he was going to shoot someone."

"He *is* crazy," Michael said.

"He isn't crazy, he's got that stress syndrome," Shae told him. "He's stored all these violent memories, and situations like that trigger them. It's like he's back in the war, even though he's not."

"If that's not crazy, what is?" Michael asked.

That was one of the questions that did not get answered that summer. The veteran kept largely to himself. Sometimes he exploded in rage inside the cabin, yelling and smacking the walls with his fists, and he always kept an eye out for danger, but he was not the only one in Garden Court to do so that summer. I had done it most of my life. I felt an empathy for the veteran, a strange empathy since I had never fought in a war nor seen battle. Maybe his utter aloneness spoke to me, his isolation inside himself, his porous borders where past seeped into present and made itself at home there.

The local paper carried a notice reminding residents of the final deadline for filing applications for Natural Disaster

Relief. Officials had pushed the deadline several times and each time they warned of the finality of the new deadline and each time new extensions followed. This time, the newspaper advised, the deadline was final except for individual extensions for good cause, and, anyway, the editor said, people should be anxious to get their money and put the whole thing behind them.

Shae applied for a good cause extension but received a flat rejection, so she spent the final days before the deadline re-evaluating her losses and obtaining additional replacement estimates. She would sit on the deck and work on the application while I weeded flower beds. When she concentrated hard, she stuck out her tongue, stretching it up toward her nose.

"Receipts," she complained. "They want receipts. If water covers your house, what are the odds of having saved your receipts? Why doesn't someone use their head now and then?"

Larry did not intend to fill out a separate form because most of the items destroyed in the cabin belonged to Shae. If she received the amount requested, she would give him five hundred dollars. I asked him what he would do with the money and he had it all planned out: he would get his dentures fixed and buy a steak and eat it.

Michael's mother sent in his application for natural disaster relief promptly, so his check arrived before Shae dropped her application in the mail. Michael strutted around Garden Court when his check arrived, bragging about it to Shae, but his mother, his legal guardian, would not cash it until she cleared it with the Lord first. That

Tuesday afternoon she sat with Michael at the picnic table talking in low, serious tones, while Shae puttered about the deck listening to as much as she could catch. After Michael's mother left to buy his food for the week, Shae made a beeline for Michael.

"What did you lose?" she demanded.

"I had this stereo before the flood, but these guys stole it," he said.

"You can't claim it then," Shae told him.

"But I knew who took it so I might have got it back if the flood hadn't ruined it."

Shae extended her lips and scowled. "Why didn't you call the cops if you knew who stole it?" she demanded.

Michael's eyes widened. He exhaled long and slow and backed away from Shae onto the safety of his own cabin steps, as if even the notion of calling the police might bring hellfire upon him.

All I knew about the natural disaster aid program was that it wasn't likely to cover whatever had happened to me. Still, when Michael's mother wanted advice about the natural disaster aid program, it was to me she turned.

I was clipping faded camellias off a bush one Tuesday when Michael's mother passed through the trellis and walked directly over to me. The smell of flowers was everywhere, and silky pink petals adorned the earth around my knees, but she jumped right in with her legal question: could the loss of Michael's stereo be rightfully claimed as a natural disaster? As I sat there looking at her, clippers still in my hand, she pulled out a pocket dictionary and went through the arguments. "Disaster" was easy enough, she said, since it implied misfortune and distress.

Shae, listening from the deck as attentively as any Supreme Court justice, declared the term broad enough to encompass the flood and the theft or either one alone. But that was not enough, she said. She hurried down, grabbed the dictionary and looked up "natural." This was less certain. The definition, "present in or produced by nature," seemed to include every action under the sun but of course it could not since some things were unnatural. Michael's mother looked up "unnatural," and it said "violating natural law, inhuman."

"It's normal to steal stuff," Michael said. "Lots of people steal stuff so it can't be inhuman."

Shae pointed out that only humans do inhuman things–you would never say a bear acted inhumanely, for example, and that just because many people did something would not make it natural.

"And anyway," Michael's mother said to Michael in a shrill voice, "most people don't steal. Most people wouldn't consider stealing." She looked over at Shae for support, but Shae said, "Hah, that's news to me," and offered Michael a cigarette.

Michael did not smoke as much as Shae, but he still went through a pack a day and he drank at night, almost every night, while his money lasted. The liquor store was two blocks from Garden Court on the corner of River Road and Church and Michael would dress for these outings in heavy layers of clothing as if he were preparing to walk through a blizzard. He knew several young boys who drank but were too young to buy liquor and when he did not have money to buy beer, he would take their money and buy beer for them and keep one-third of it. He was a hard businessman. After his disaster check cleared and he had extra cash every week for beer, he increased his cut of the boys' beer to fifty percent since he was not desperate for it. There must have been some other source since they did not come around as often after the rate increase.

As summer ripened, morning dawned earlier, and daylight lingered of an evening. Everyone relaxed into the rhythm. The long hours of sunshine seemed enough to protect us all from harm, and the old fears and precautions faded.

Without further reflection, I bought a red collar for the dog at Safeway. Then I bought a silver tag at the hardware store and had them inscribe it "Brutus." The dog sat patiently as I attached the tag to the collar with a little metal loop and buckled the collar around his neck, then he jumped to his feet and shook his head. The tag jingled against the buckle of the collar. He shook again, harder, and then pranced up and down the footpath.

Larry wandered out of his cabin in the late morning, his dark hair and beard mussed and his shirt still unbuttoned. The dog sprinted over to him, stretching out his neck and shaking the collar.

"Nice collar Big B," Larry said, nodding. He patted the dog's head.

A while later, Michael carried his lunch plate to the picnic table. Brutus lay in a sunny spot on the footpath not far from where I was working, but he leaped to his feet and bounded over to the boy, placing his front paws on the bench.

"None for you," the boy said, putting his back between the dog and his lunch. Brutus retreated immediately.

"He's showing you his collar," Larry said from the deck.

"Oh, hey, let's see old boy." Michael turned around and called him. The dog returned head stretched high. His ears stood up sometimes like cow ears, even the torn one. Michael carefully inspected the collar and read the little tag.

"That's nice, Bru," he finally pronounced. "Red looks nice."

The dog gave his head a shake, jiggling the tag. Then he pranced up the footpath, found a loose stick, and carried it over to drop it at Larry's feet.

Larry gazed down at the stick for a few minutes, then picked it up and threw it. It did not go very far, but the dog sprang to life. He sped up the footpath, skidding and tumbling in the dirt. When he stood up, he had the stick in his mouth. He trotted back to Larry and dropped it at his feet again.

"Wow," Larry said.

"Do it again," Michael told him. He rose and carried his plate over to the steps of the deck. They did it again and again. I kept working until that scent reappeared suddenly like some potent flower essence all around me, strong and willful on the light breeze. I stopped working then and moved into the sunshine near Larry and Michael and Brutus. They played and played, and I sat on that redwood deck and watched. Summer was everywhere. The wood was warm, like living flesh.

CHAPTER 9

BY THE TIME Shae's disability appeal came to hearing, the vine had topped the Garden Court trellis and exploded into tiny white stars of jasmine. I could smell the fragrance halfway up to the cafe.

Shae spent the afternoon before the hearing out in the courtyard talking with Michael's mother.

"That doctor, how can he live with himself?" Shae said. "To sit there and lie – a doctor! – and say that it's me that's lying. My word against his. Hah! Who do you think they're going to believe?"

Michael's mother also distrusted the hearing process and talked about the trauma of Michael's conservatorship hearing. Their family psychiatrist told the court under oath that Michael never said a word during his therapy sessions, and he diagnosed him as a schizophrenic and a pathological liar. The judge asked how he determined Michael was a liar if he did not talk at all and almost threw the parents out of court on that basis. I considered it a valid objection, perhaps because I too had been the family liar, but Michael's mother did not see it that way.

"As if the testimony of family didn't count," she said with a sigh. "Everyone knows how hard it is to diagnose schizophrenia. The psychiatrist explained that schizophrenics see and believe things that others do not – like Michael phoning the police to say his father was trying to kill him. His father, a minister of God! Thank heavens Michael's brother explained how he lies. During the commitment, Michael became autistic. He's doing better now."

"My doctor's gonna get hit with a suit if he isn't careful," Shae said. "He's violating his duty and his responsibility."

Shae left for the hearing the next morning early. I wished her luck and watched her lug the heavy briefcase past the dark cabins. Her chances of winning were small. But later that afternoon, she trotted up the footpath shouting the news: she'd won the appeal. The court tossed out the decision against her on the grounds of discovery abuse and ordered a new hearing. Michael and Larry stopped their game of checkers to clap and everyone congratulated her. The dog began jumping about barking at the noise and Shae offered round cigarettes and even Vama came out, a dishtowel draped over one shoulder. Shae told the story of the hearing from start to finish, who said what and how she responded. We all patted her on the back and said she would win rehab in the end. She said she would study to be a paralegal and work on cases just like this one, buy a little house and grow tomatoes in the hot sun.

After Larry and Michael moved inside to watch

Columbo, Shae asked me about discovery abuse. I explained that the law required all parties in a case to share whatever evidence they found with the other side on the theory that only by knowing the whole truth could a matter be adjudged. This exchange of evidence was called "discovery." You got in trouble for keeping the other side in the dark. Shae jotted down notes on a little yellow pad as I spoke, and then borrowed a few of my law books to bone up for the next hearing.

Shae's victory gave us a sense that the worst times were over, that things might all work out after all. I mistrusted this optimism, yet problems seemed to evaporate before my eyes. Trees and flowers thrived, and sunshine slanted farther into the corners of Garden Court each day. Morning after morning I checked my heart and found it clear of darkness; as the nightmares eased, the idea of ending my life began to seem silly, the product of an over-active imagination. It occurred to me that I spent half of the previous year worried about dying and the other half planning to kill myself. I'd never viewed it that way before and it made me laugh.

But other things did not work out, like finding the dog Brutus a home. My lost-and-found ad expired, and the paper did not allow me to renew it. "If nobody claims something after four weeks, it's clearly been dumped," the lady told me. Larry suggested we put up a "free pit bull" sign on the community bulletin board at the cafe, but Shae nixed it. With all the crazies on the river in the summer, she said, the dog would likely end up in bad hands.

The newspaper ran a series of articles on organized dog fighting and the increasing number of stolen dogs in the region, mostly pit bulls and Rottweilers. Sometimes small dogs and cats disappeared too, stolen for bait to train the fighting dogs to kill. One article talked about men who stage dog fights for wagering, saying that fights occurred in every part of the country including the River. The paper quoted a local man under privacy guarantees who described it as a sport like any other and assured the reporter that the dogs fought each other because they loved it, not because of anything the dogmen did. He said that dogmen held jobs and paid taxes and saluted the flag like other respectable citizens and shouldn't have the use of their own property restricted.

Another article explained the difficulty of cracking down on dog fighting, a crime committed in the shadows of the community. Under current law, the article said, the police could only arrest a dog fighter if they caught him with his pants down, so to speak, in the middle of a fight. This rarely happened. If an unfamiliar face showed up at a fight, the men disappeared into the night leaving behind dogs and fighting paraphernalia.

The article featured a local policeman and ran his picture. I knew him, a hefty man who sat in the cafe mornings eating donuts. He said that fights were gruesome but rare on the River, and that the few actual cases involved a foreign element.

I kept my eyes on the Mexicans next door, but no more dogfights took place there. The men still drank beer out in their yard on Sunday afternoons and played loud music, but, with the good weather, everybody else did the same thing. One time I heard noises over there and climbed up the ladder to peer over the fence. One of the men was playing ball with a child and they both looked up and waved.

One afternoon, another group of day-laborers arrived in the neighborhood. I was out back dumping garbage when a pick-up truck pulled slowly up the dirt alley behind Garden Court, raising a cloud of dust behind it. It stopped just up the road, and a dozen men jumped out of the back, calling to each other in Spanish. They unloaded bed rolls and bulging, brightly colored plastic bags, then hauled them back through the mulch on the far side of the dirt alley. Shae said there was an apartment building back there but it had been condemned after the flood. I could just make out the outline of it when I walked down that dirt alley to the abandoned park.

I passed the abandoned park every day on my way back from the cafe. Each time I felt the dark pull of the amphitheater back in the woods, the strange familiarity of that walk, the empty altar. I could not shake it. One cloudless morning I decided to return there. It seemed safe, the new grass in the park glittered with dew. White blossoms floated in small clouds above the gnarled branches of the apple tree. Even the crumbling wall marking the west border of the field overflowed with blackberry vines. Behind it and beyond, the deep shadow of the forest stood silent, waiting.

The tramp Michael lounged on the bench under the apple tree, his dog Mollybelle at his feet. He rubbed a sunken chest with the back of one hand.

"Good morning Michael," I called out.

He looked at me darkly for a long moment, then spat on the ground. "Yes, lass, it's a good morning," he said, precisely and with great bitterness. "It's a good morning, if you're not a drunk."

This seemed a bad omen and I did not risk a walk into the shadowy wood but returned to Garden Court to fertilize the thin bush outside my window. No flower buds grew on its branches, but a few soft leaves appeared, and fragile new shoots. I hadn't had any of those episodes in weeks, and once I left a front window open a crack all night long. The pit bull slept on a blanket outside my door and would give warning, I figured, of invaders or marauders or thieves in the night.

I set out dry food for the pit bull every morning. Sometimes I fed Butterball from next door too. The puppy grew larger every day and ate anything it came across. One day it could no longer wedge its chubby body through the hole in the fence between its yard and Garden Court. I heard pitiful yips and rushed out expecting to see the shadow dog, but it was only Butterball, stuck halfway through the hole in the fence. I pushed him back to his own side, and the pup trotted around and came merrily up the footpath from Fourth Street. But by the time the dog headed home, it forgot the dangers of the shortcut and again its squeals filled the courtyard. When this happened a third time, I asked Jack the maintenance man to board over the hole.

Butterball did not take this personally. Many mornings the pup wandered through the jasmine trellis and up the footpath. Although he was bigger than Brutus already, he still looked like a puppy with that foolish fluffy head and big paws. He came for the pit bull and together they would run out the back entrance of Garden Court. Late afternoon the two returned together, muddy and tired, their tongues hanging low, mouths pulled back in that way that makes dogs look like they are smiling.

Michael and Larry played checkers and watched for the dogs to return. They saved little snacks for them. Michael always divided the treat carefully into two equal amounts, but Larry just tossed something out and hoped each got some. One day Shae returned from her storage unit with her mum's bone china soup terrine and we kept it beside the picnic table with water for the dogs.

The pit bull Brutus relaxed into the new season. He no longer positioned himself alone in the middle of the footpath, muscles coiled to leap up and away in case of trouble. Most of the time he wedged himself into a spot of sunlight near the picnic table and would wag his tail slightly, tentatively, whenever one of us came near.

The dog hung around so much that the cooking lady complained, and management came over to find out whether someone was harboring a dog against the rules of Garden Court. Shae was sitting on the deck sorting papers for her disability hearing. She jumped up and started in, how the residents of Garden Court had complained time after time to management about the pit bull, fully expecting and rightly expecting management to act quickly to protect them and yet management had done nothing. They were always going on about how the vet that owned the place did not want the residents to keep pets, but they wouldn't lift a finger to get rid of the vicious strays! Shae had told them someone was going to get bit someday and the receptionist had responded "better you than me, honey."

"Better you than me, honey," Shae repeated in a loud,

bitter voice from her post on the deck. "And now you come over here and accuse me of harboring an illegal dog, a dog we've been complaining about for weeks."

This approach worked well enough even though Brutus was sitting next to Larry the whole time with that basin of water set out for him. Shae considered the matter a victory, but management must have called the pound again because the following day, after Shae left for her meeting, the dogcatcher came back. The afternoon was bright and quiet, and we heard the squeal of brakes and the stomping footsteps before we saw the man. The dog ran to slide through the hole in the fence, but the board was nailed over it, so he was cornered there where my cabin met the fence. The dogcatcher carried a long pole with a clip on the end and spray to subdue the dog and Brutus sat in the corner with his ears pulled way back so it looked like he did not have ears at all, just a round skull and huge dark eyes. Michael vanished like an angel and Larry ducked inside his cabin and closed the door.

I was standing by my kitchen door and the dogcatcher was on me in a minute. He leaned toward me and the smell of old cigarette smoke spilled over me, reminding me of my father's pipe. He began talking in a loud voice. He had been called before the supervisor and it was not going to happen again. Dog fighting was on the rise on the river. The county's policy was to get rid of stray pit bulls and, pursuant to this policy, it was exercising its right to put this dog down. Only the owner had the right to interfere. I said nothing. I could not have spoken if my life depended on it.

He turned to the dog then. The little dog tried to edge

away, and the man snorted a laugh. He lit a cigarette and held it in his mouth while he approached the dog. "You got nowhere to go," he said to the dog, laughing a little. "You're all mine."

At these words, that weird feeling settled over me again, like I was watching the scene on television and not there at all, floating, floating somewhere above. From a distance, I saw the man drag deep on his cigarette, then throw it to the ground, twist it out with his boot. I saw him approach the dog, heard him chuckle. I slipped further away, out of my body, and I could not move, not an arm, not a leg. I could not operate my body anymore. It was a lifeless mass below me and I floated over it like a ghost.

From far away I saw the dog realize he was trapped, saw his body begin to tremble, saw his eyes turn toward me, not asking for help, just a quick look. But as his wide eyes met mine, a heat started to rise in me, coming up fast like fire whooshes up a dry tree, rising in a wave of heat from my feet to my face, pushing my lip up in a sort of snarl. Suddenly I was back in my body, I could move, and my arm shot out and flung open my kitchen door with a clack like gunfire, and the dog was up and inside the house and I slammed the door and stood in front of it, my foot tapping in a spastic rhythm, adrenalin shooting fire crackers all around the courtyard.

The man started yelling but I did not move, just stood there in front of that door, watching his face twist up and his mouth open and shut and that cigarette fall to the ground. For a few minutes I burned with energy like a torch, then the heat passed and the strength passed too, leaving me empty. He could have knocked me over with a feather. He could have walked right in.

But he did not try to get in. He wrote me out a ticket for having a dog without a license and another for having a dog without a rabies tag and talked rough and angry for a long time. He said that pits were bad, impervious to pain, demon dogs with jaws that locked and a taste for blood. He said that the dog would get me, that it would wait until I was asleep and then rip me open, that I would not be safe in my own bed. Then he said I would have to keep that dog inside all day, every day, because he, the dogcatcher, would be back when I least expected it, even at night when he was off work, and he would get that dog, he swore he would get him. And he would get me too.

As soon as he had gone, my teeth started chattering and my hands started shaking and the whole scene zoomed away again until I was watching it from somewhere above my head. Disconnected images flooded my brain, the mottled sheets, moonlight, my sister's little face. I knew that I was really going crazy this time, that the craziness has overtaken me once and for all and there was nothing I could do to save myself.

I staggered into my cabin and sank to the floor and there was the dog, curled up in a corner on a towel. The dog's ears had disappeared, glued tight to his skull, and his eyes shone huge and deep like craters. His entire body shivered violently like it was hooked up to a vibrating machine. I watched him for a few minutes, then I moved over next to him into a patch of sunshine slanting in from the kitchen window. I stroked his little head over and over and said I would not let them get him, and he finally stopped shaking and went to sleep. I got up and made myself coffee. Somewhere in the middle of drinking it, I realized that the round was over and I was still standing.

That night when I made up my mattress on the floor of the living room, I tried to figure out what to do with the pit bull. He clearly could not pass the night outside because of the dogcatcher, but where to put him? The kitchen was the logical place, but no door separated the kitchen and the front room where I slept on the floor and, after all, the dog was a pit bull. Finally I settled the dog in the kitchen on a blanket, then piled up objects from the back room in the doorway to block it: boxes of law books, a chair, a suitcase, then stacked pots and pans on top to make noise if he tried anything. I lay down to sleep and dreamed there was a bogeyman in the house after me, a bogeyman in my own house trying to kill me, but nobody believed me because he was invisible. He only became visible if two people happened to look right where he was at exactly the same moment, the crossing lines of their vision pinpointing him like the reticle on a rifle scope.

When I woke up, I remembered in a rush that the pit bull spent the night in my house, and I jerked my eyes over to make sure that the barricade was in place. It was still there. The panic dissipated in the cool clear air of morning. Suddenly I became aware of a warm heaviness against the back of my knees and I sat up quickly: There was the little pit bull, curled tight at the foot of the bed. He looked up at me wide-eyed, waiting for something terrible to happen.

CHAPTER 10

THE CLEAN-UP COMMITTEE postponed its barbeque so often that Shae said it would double as a Christmas party, but finally it was announced for one Saturday in early summer. Along with the free food, the fair was to have live music, a flea market and booths sponsored by town merchants. Clean-Up Week banners reappeared on River Road and this time nobody touched them.

The morning of the barbeque was cool and fresh, but the sky was cloudless, promising a sunny afternoon. On my way back to Garden Court, I circled around by Safeway parking lot. Big garbage cans stood sentry on either side of the car entryway with red plastic ribbon strung between them. In the lot, men and women were setting up flea market booths, locking into place the legs of fold-up tables, unloading boxes. No merchants were there yet, but a crew of firemen were building a stage at the far west side of the lot. A little farther down, more firemen rolled king-size metal barbeques into a neat line.

Shae spotted me the minute I passed the Garden Court

trellis. "Hey there," she called. "Here's the Clean Up Fair activities. Food's not 'til noon, but music starts at eleven." She waved a program in the air in my direction so enthusiastically that she lost her grip and it wafted to the ground near the picnic table. Michael snatched it up and squinted at it, patting Brutus with one hand.

"Look, Brutus," Michael said, positioning the program before the dog's face and pointing. "The vet's giving rabies shots for a dollar."

Shae frowned and sniffed disdainfully. "If it's the jerk that owns Garden Court, I'm going to give him a piece of my mind," she said. "What kind of a vet would say his tenants couldn't keep pets? But I've heard he's got his son working there, used to be a priest of all things. All they need now is the holy ghost to work nights and weekends."

I rolled out the hose and began my usual garden chores with an increasing audience as, little by little, the other residents came out of the cabins and into the sunshine. Michael and Larry played checkers at the picnic table, while Vama crocheted in a chair on the deck. Even old Grover appeared, escorted outside by his visiting nurse. The veteran and his mother left for the fair early so they could eat and leave before the crowds, and Felicia also hurried off to set up a fortune-telling booth. On her way out, she promised us a special rate: two readings for the price of one.

After a while, a voice floated over from the Safeway lot, someone saying "one, two, three" into a microphone. Soon music starting up, then the shuffle and chatter of people walking up Fourth toward Safeway. Shae decided to dress for the event, a lengthy process, but she finally appeared wearing a loose summer dress and a floppy purple hat. I tied a cord to the dog's collar and headed out with Shae toward the fair.

Even as we passed the post office, a wave of noise and activity broke over us. The Safeway parking lot buzzed with shouts and laughter. As we drew closer, we could see the stage platform at the back where band members arranged an electric keyboard and set up drums. Shae nudged me and pointed out the Garden Court maintenance man, Jack, tuning his guitar in the shade of the stage.

"Funny, the way he didn't remember fixing my wiring," Shae said. "Alkies have blackouts all the time, but Jack's not a drinker. One of the few on the river."

Jack sat stolidly on the steps to the stage, completely blocking the path. Two young men waited to pass but he did not even glance their way. Shae rolled her eyes, then began to tell me about different times she'd blacked out before she stopped drinking, how she would come to in a strange room and try to piece together what had happened from all available clues.

"It's not like fainting," she told me. "When you faint, you just lie there in one place until you come to again. When you black out, you keep on doing things, lots of things, things you probably wouldn't do sober, but when the blackout passes, you can't remember anything about what you did. Those memories are just gone."

She made a wry face and nodded grimly. "Like this one time I came out of a blackout and I was in my own bed. The last thing I remembered was leaving work Friday, but the TV says it's Saturday afternoon. My head feels like someone is beating it with a hammer, so I go over to the corner bar for some hair of the dog. When I walk in, all the regulars start clapping. Turns out I'd spent most of the night there, dancing naked on a table."

I tried to picture this as we wandered up and down the aisles of the fair, but the idea of being locked out of your own memories brought both claustrophobia and vertigo at the same time, like being wrapped too tightly in a blanket and tossed off a cliff. But the images of Shae's story quickly gave way to the kaleidoscope of smells and colors of the fair. Smoke rose in puffy clouds from the barbeques, mixing with the meaty smell of sizzling hot dogs. Young firemen in aprons flipped the hotdogs, laughing and joking with the hungry crowd, while dressed-up church ladies rolled out paper for tablecloths on the long, sawhorse-and-plank tables, taping down the edges. Other ladies set out glass jars full of paper napkins on the tables and squeeze bottles of ketchup and mustard.

The flea market tables lined River Road, the local business booths nearer to the stage. The cafe booth offered coffee and soft drinks, a quarter a cup. Shae and I each bought a coffee and stood looking around. In the booth beside us, the county library offered used paperbacks, ten for a dollar. The hardware store booth stood beside a table run by lawyers offering free legal advice. Across the way, the battered women's shelter shared table space with the Mental Health Center. Their sign said: "What you pretend didn't happen yesterday will happen again tomorrow."

I spotted a booth with a handwritten sign taped to the edge of the table: "*Bordeaux Vet Clinic, rabies shots $1.00.*"

Someone had drawn smiling faces into the 0s. Already a dozen people waited in line with their pets. Shae trotted off to say hello at the AA booth and I stepped into the line at the vet's booth behind a young lady with two cat carriers.

It was not unpleasant to wait. The sun topped the redwoods, warm and friendly in the wide blue sky, and I saw people I recognized. The cooking lady walked by with her kids and said hi, then I saw Robbie talking to Shae at the AA booth and they both waved to me. The band started playing "Proud Mary" and I caught myself singing under my breath, "rolling, rolling, rolling on the river."

When the lady in front of me reached the top of the line, I got a look at the vet wiping down the examination table with large, easy movements. It was the same young guy who opened the clinic every morning. He wore jeans and a Clean-Up Week T-shirt. Up close, he still looked like a Ken Doll except for the gold earring in his left ear.

He finished his task and turned to the cat lady. "Hi, I'm Jeff Bordeaux," he said. His blue eyes shone bright but dreamy, slightly unfocussed like in pictures of Jesus as a boy, but you could not miss his powerful physical presence. The girl leaned toward him, tipping her head so that her hair fell in a wave across her cheek. She murmured something I did not hear, and the man laughed. "Fill dad's shoes? Not likely," he said. "I just give him a hand at the clinic."

The girl batted her lashes at him as she slid a cat carrier across the table. "So, *you* have to work Saturdays while *he* plays golf?" she teased.

"Hey," the vet protested, frowning slightly. "Even Dad can't be everywhere at once. His specialty has always been livestock, so I do the small animal work." A new tightness appeared in his voice, shading it just a little, but the girl noticed.

"Now I've made you angry," she pouted.

"Anger is not a big part of my life," he said emphatically. "And besides," he added, smiling, "there is some chance that dad is on the greens even as we speak."

He turned to the cats, then, just making small talk as he opened the carriers. He extracted the reluctant cats one by one, examined them and gave the injections, while the owner chatted with him, batted her eyes and smiled radiantly. She paid her two dollars, then tossed her hair for him one last time as she walked away, but the vet's eyes did not follow her; they turned to the next animal in line: Brutus.

I stepped toward the table, but Brutus pulled back on the rope, turning his head away. As he did, I saw as if for the first time his ravaged skin, the sores, the scars; how his ribs stuck out of his thin body like the frame of a covered wagon. The vet came around from behind the table. Even as he squatted down and put out his right hand toward Brutus, I could feel his presence like a gravitational field overlapping my own, neither stronger nor weaker, the same tone, same color. The vet, however, did not notice. His eyes locked on Brutus.

"Hey old fellow," he said. "I'm not going to hurt you." Brutus walked closer slowly and finally allowed the vet to pat his head and lift him to the examination table.

The vet rubbed the dog's ears before he began the routine examination: eyes, nose, teeth, ears. "Christ," he said under his breath. His fingers explored the dog's ribs, and then lifted each leg, flexing it gently at the knee. When he finished, he turned his eyes toward me slowly.

"He's just over a year old and I would have given him ten," he said. He spoke in a low voice only I could hear; it held no overt judgment, but the gray eyes pierced me. "What did you do to this dog?" he asked.

I just looked at him hard without saying a word. After a few minutes, he said, "Okay then, who did what to this dog?"

"I don't know," I said. I used to know everything, but here was yet another question to which I had no answer. I wondered when my life had turned into a jigsaw puzzle with all the important pieces missing, but I did not know that answer either.

I looked up and found the vet still watching me; he held my gaze for a long moment as if seeking answers in my eyes. Finally he asked, "How did you come by this dog?"

I took a deep breath. "He was there," I said, shrugging. I felt the shadow of something pass over me. "His heart was broken," I said. I heard my voice cracking and stopped. The vet looked away from me then, down past the dog's head.

"This dog's been fought," he said in the same, neutral voice. "And he's been hurt. Not too bad, considering the spectrum of what's possible, but bad enough: ears ripped, ribs broken, scarring." He inspected Brutus again. "Aggressive toward other dogs? Cats?"

I shook my head.

"Some aren't, no matter what they go through, unless another dog attacks. Or maybe he was a blood," he said, "used to train the fighters." He thought about it a bit, stroking Brutus. "This guy's small but tough, real tough I would say, too tough for a blood."

His eyes found the dog's name tag. "Et tu Brutus?" he said softly, bending close to the brown eyes. "What did they do to you friend?" The dog sat down and stared unwavering at the man with wide, trusting eyes. Then, with great dignity, he offered the vet his front right paw.

The man took the paw and held it gently. His face twisted as if he were in pain, and he passed his hand over his eyes, letting out a long breath through his nose. But when he spoke again, his voice was light. "Jesus, it still gets me," he said. "Dad says it's part of a vet's life, you have to get used to it. And he's right." He nodded agreement with his father's words but as he turned to prepare the injection, his jaw was still set hard. "But I'm not quite there yet," he muttered under his breath.

The shot only took a moment; Brutus did not move or make a sound when the needle punctured his skin. The vet rubbed the dog's ears one more time then set him on the ground.

"Listen," the vet told me as he set the dog on the ground. "Brutus has a bad skin infection. Bring him by the clinic next week and I'll test him, treat him. Free," he added, low, looking both ways as he said it, and then nodding at me encouragingly. I handed him a dollar bill, but he pushed it back at me.

"It's my own private rebellion," he said, winking, as if it were a joke. "Won't you let me help this dog?" I felt his energy again, warm and electric where it touched mine, and I glanced up sharply, but his eyes held only the simple question.

Back on the ground, Brutus wagged his tail and pranced around as we wandered around the fair. I caught sight of Shae at the free legal advice booth, then lost her in the crowd. As I sifted through used books, I saw Michael and Larry walking up from River Road. Michael wore a sweatshirt with the hood drawn up so far it shadowed his face and he trotted along, his hands plunged deep in his pockets. Larry ambled well behind him, smiling and nodding happily at all the activity, while Michael turned back nervously every few seconds to hurry him along.

When Michael spotted me, he hurried over. He took his hands from his pocket to pat the dog. Larry strolled in a few minutes later. Both he and Michael bought cokes from the cafe stand, then we all went over to the barbeque area and found Shae already in line with Robbie, holding a place for us.

Robbie led the way through the food line. I went through after Shae, and Larry and Michael followed. Town ladies handed out flimsy paper plates, and we piled on hot dogs, beans and coleslaw. My plate wobbled so I held it with one palm underneath and followed Shae to an empty table. The five of us took up most of the table space and Brutus settled in the shade underneath. The sun shone warm and welcoming and even Michael lowered his hood and glanced around. People walked by and said hello and we ate the free food happily.

Life seemed to pause in that moment, and everything seemed fine, funny. Michael fed the last section of his hot dog to Brutus, then he started making up silly knock-knock jokes and someone sent Larry over a big bottle of coke. Then Shae tried to fix the ketchup bottle and accidentally squirted ketchup over her face. We all laughed, even Shae. As she wiped her face with the tiny paper napkins, her hat fell off and her hot dog slid off her plate onto the ground where Brutus gulped it down quickly and we laughed more. It felt that nothing funnier had happened since the world began.

Larry was seated between Robbie and Michael. As Shae went back to the line to get another hot dog, he turned to Robbie and asked kindly: "So how are you, Robbie?"

"I am just fine, Larry," she said and smiled at him. She said something about George, but I couldn't hear because the music started up. This time it was Jack, playing the guitar and singing one of his very long songs. After the song, a fireman stepped out and introduced Jack, presenting him as "a young River man, going places." Just then Shae returned with a whole platter of hot dogs and served us all seconds, and we ate and listened to Jack and laughed at almost anything at all.

Shae knew where Felicia had set up her fortune telling booth so when we finished eating, she led us over to see what the stars foretold. The booth consisted of a card table with a chair on each side. A sign taped to the front edge of the table said: "White Rose Readings - $2.00" and a vase on the table contained one white rose. The client chair was empty, so Shae sat in it and plunked down two dollars for her and Larry. Felicia brought out a sheet of paper printed with a large circle divided into twelve slices like a pie. She wrote Shae's name and birth information on the top. After that, she looked in a thick book she kept beside her and jotted down symbols into some of the pie slices, muttering to herself in Spanish. Bent over the horoscope like that she looked like a gypsy shrouded in veils and her darkness took on a mystery and intensity, the crazed lines on her brow smoothed into an almost immortal face. You had to remember that it was just Felicia, who rented the cabin on Fourth Street, Felicia, whose daughter lived with the mortician.

Felicia lifted up the vase with the rose in it and set it down in the center of Shae's chart. She closed her eyes and waved her right hand in the air in front of Shae making large S's. Then she cupped her hands around the flower without touching it.

"Your road has not been easy," she said without opening her eyes. "Someone took something from you. You fight to get it back."

"My aunts?" Shae cut in. "It's my aunts!"

Felicia said she saw a powerful woman, represented by Shae's moon in Scorpio, a powerful woman who would haunt her all her life. She told her other things as well, of bad luck turning to good, of financial hurdles, of opportunities coming. In time, Felicia opened her eyes, squinted, and swept the air in front of her with her hands as if to clear Shae out. Shae stood up and moved off, looking dazed, while Felicia beckoned toward the open chair.

Larry backed away a few steps, so I sat down. Felicia did a chart, then started with the S's but after trying them several times, she shook her head, the peaceful look on her face changing to a darker one that bordered on anger. She turned to my chart, then, and said I was born into the house of death, the eighth house of death and sex and regeneration, that my life was a battlefield. Everyone looked at me. I thought the battlefield image silly, as if I went to war like the veteran after all, but nothing Felicia said seemed to matter much or change anything, so I listened until she stopped talking. After that, neither Michael nor Larry wanted a reading, so I paid up a dollar to Shae and we hurried off in the other direction.

"No wonder there was no line," Shae joked, once we moved well out of earshot.

"Stars can't tell things like that," jeered Michael. "Stars don't tell you anything except where they used to be. You know that some of the stars in the sky burned out thousands of years ago?"

Larry thought about this. "Then why do we still see them?" he asked, at last.

"The light takes so long to get here," Michael said. "Maybe they gave off that light a million years ago and since then got hauled away somewhere."

"Or died," Larry said.

"Or died," Michael allowed. "So here they're signaling to us, but they aren't around anymore. I saw that on TV last night."

Larry pondered this in silence. "Well," he said finally. "That's too bad."

Around five o'clock, things started breaking up. Larry and Michael headed back to Garden Court to catch Columbo, but I wanted to take Brutus for some exercise and Shae came with me. The music trailed us a long way up River Road west, carried on a warm breeze. We stopped at a clearing near the river and I threw the tennis ball. It bounced high and Brutus leaped to catch it, bringing it back to me joyfully, at a run. The sky was a high blue with banked clouds in the west. Shae lit a cigarette, blew the smoke out thoughtfully.

"I think it's my mum that haunts me," Shae told me. "What Felicia said. I think that's my mum; she shows up all the time in my dreams. I worked on it during the eighth step in AA, but with mum you could never really make amends. She never forgave anything." In the silence, I threw the ball again, then again. Brutus ran, jumped and snatched it out of the air every time as if it could save his life.

"My childhood was a disaster," Shae continued. "I guess yours was too."

I shook my head, turning to her and frowning slightly. "Not at all," I said, shrugging. "I'll show you some photos." Even to my ear it sounded weak. I threw the ball as far as I could, my arm burning from the effort.

"I had a fairytale childhood," I added firmly, but still I wasn't certain; was it fairytale childhood or storybook childhood? I tried out both of them to myself, but both sounded familiar. "Anyway," I said, nodding, "a perfect childhood."

Shae looked over at me sharply, eyes narrowed.

I threw the ball again hard and it soared high on the bounce. Beyond the clearing, the river lay dark and sluggish, more a dead snake than a living body of water winding its way down to the ocean. I tried to remember something from my childhood, anything other than the photos, but there was only fog. All I could pull up was my sister's face, her eyes. Finally, I shrugged again.

"Okay," Shae said briskly, "a fairytale childhood. But which fairytale do you have in mind?"

A few nights later, I heard someone under my cabin trying to kill me. I was sleeping on the floor as usual, the dog at my feet, when a hollow, banging noise came from somewhere in or near my cabin. I woke up instantly, every muscle in my body tensed, listening, straining to hear. I knew it was very late since I could not hear television noise from any of the cabins. I listened intently to the silence.

There was nothing for a long time, only my own listening, active as motion. Then a dull bang from under the floor where I lay, a little to my left. The dog heard it too. His head lifted, ears high. He lay like a sphinx, listening, trembling slightly. I watched the clock's minute hand change, five minutes passed, then ten. Suddenly something banged dully under the floor, a little to the left of the mattress. Another bang. There was someone under my cabin.

Even as I listened, my mind surged forward with contingency plans. The locks on both doors opened with the same key, a key currently under my pillow. I reached for it and touched it, cold and real. The one duplicate key lay in my jeans pocket. No other keys existed so he couldn't get in the doors. If he tried the window, I kept that iron pipe beside the refrigerator.

Brutus growled very low in the back of his throat almost like a cat, and his body was trembling. Another banging noise from under the house, the other side this time, muffled, like someone trying not to make noise. Then a scuffling. I reached for my green flashlight and turned it on, scanning the room.

What was he doing under the house? How could he get at me from under the house? My eyes swept the floorboards for a saw or drill cutting through from below like you see in cartoons. Suddenly it occurred to me that he might not be trying to get in, he might be trying something else: it might be fire, it might be explosives. The panic crashed over me. Here I was ready for forced entry, but it might be different. My heart pounded in my ears. The dog sat up, growling low. Then I saw the telephone: I could call the police. Someone was breaking into my house; I could call the police. It was normal to call the police if someone was breaking into your house. I reached for the phone.

I heard the siren some minutes later, then heard heavy footsteps up the pathway. I crept out of bed and peered out the front window. Two flashlight beams swept up the Garden Court footpath. I slipped on shoes, unlocked the door and went out, the dog close beside me.

There were two policemen, one heavy-set with his stomach pushing hard against his holster, the other taller, thinner, with a mustache. They came up the footpath fast, not running but almost.

"Someone breaking into your house?" asked the heavy one. I recognized him from the coffee shop. He eyed me dubiously, my mussy braid, the sweats and T-shirt I slept in.

I explained about the noises, that it was actually under my house, the banging, the scuffling. The policemen did not say anything, but looked at each other, then at me. I explained about the dog and the dogcatcher and what he had said.

"You think the county dog catcher is under your house?" the policeman with the mustache asked, lifting his eyebrows. "At three in the morning?"

I stopped talking then. A feeling of shame came over me, an old feeling like being accused of lying as a child. But I wasn't lying now – had I truly lied as a child? I suddenly wasn't sure of anything.

"Well, we're here anyway," the other one said. "Let's take a look." They walked over to the side of my cabin. There was a crawl space between the cabin and the ground where the plumbing ran, but it did not look very big. I wished I could disappear into the air. Suddenly, there was the scuffling noise, then a series of bangs and I felt relief flood through my body, hot like whiskey.

The cop with the mustache pulled out his revolver and held it with both hands, pointing it at the hole. The heavy policeman hurried around to the other side of the cabin, near the weeping willow. I followed him, staying back toward the footpath. He had his revolver in one hand, his flashlight in his left. He turned the light toward the base of the cabin and there was a hole on that side of the house, too.

The pipes banged again, this time very loud. Something under the cabin scraped and the first policeman said, "your side," and the fat one jumped back, ready, when out from the hole came two raccoons, one after the other, eyes beady in the flashlight beam. They scooted around

Michael's cabin and out past the garbage cans on the far side of Garden Court.

The thin policemen walked around to join the other one and they both put their guns away. I did not look at them. One of them sighed. "You should get yourself a boyfriend, lady," he told me. "Something to keep you busy at night."

CHAPTER 11

WE SAT IN the cool, shifting shadow of the weeping willow through the long days of summer. If the night was foggy, as nights were from time to time as summer peaked and waned, rain would fall beneath the tree in the early morning even though the sky was clear and blue as far as you could see. I thought it was just the weeping willow and it was perhaps from this that it got its name, but old Michael told me all trees shed water in the morning after a misty night.

"Yes, they're all weeping, lass," he told me. "The trees, they never forget."

I told the others about the weeping trees and Larry and Michael both wanted to get up early to see but Michael never remembered to set his alarm clock and Larry did not have one. He asked Shae to get him up, but she said forget it: six was too early to get up to look at trees even if they were doing an Irish jig.

I always got up early, and I wasn't the only one. No matter how early I went to the cafe in the morning, the

Mexican men from across the dirt alley were already out. I would see them standing at the corner of Third Street and Armstrong Woods Road waiting for contractors who needed extra workers to stop by. Evenings they showed up again in the abandoned park, often with big dogs held on tight leads. I marked them down in my mind as possible dog fighting suspects, mostly because of the way they snuck around. But Shae said they were wary because the building they lived in had been condemned by the county since it had no water or electricity.

The week after the Clean Up Fair, I took Brutus to see the vet named Jeff. I bought a leash at Safeway in the morning, and in the afternoon, we walked up Fourth Street to the large door marked "Bordeaux Veterinary Clinic." I'd passed that door so often that it felt odd going in, like walking into a picture that's been hanging on your wall for years.

The door opened into a sterile waiting room with a beige sofa and a grouping of matching chairs around a low table; on the other side was a desk. Nobody was there. Suddenly a door in the back opened and someone poked his head out. It was Jeff.

"Hey there," he said. "I was just making coffee. Want some?" He was in jeans again, hair tousled like a choir boy, but he wore a white lab jacket. Brutus kept close to me as I followed Jeff through the examination area into a back room. It looked lived in, with a futon on the floor, books and papers piled around, a guitar in one corner. On the top of a small refrigerator was a Mr. Coffee machine, the pot half full. The room smelled warm from the coffee.

"Dad lets me use this room when I'm working late,"

Jeff said, pouring coffee into Styrofoam cups and handing me one. "At first, I actually lived here, I had so little stuff. That's the Salesians for you. We used to joke that the vow of poverty was just a ruse to cut down on closet space." He laughed, dropping easily onto the futon and signaling me to the only chair. Brutus curled up at my feet.

"Salesians?" I said.

"I was in the seminary," he told me. "For years." He riffled through a stack of papers on the floor. "Here," he said, holding one out to me. It was a photo of a half-dozen young men in long black belted robes. I picked out Jeff on the end, holding a guitar.

"Yep, that's Brother Jeff," he said. "That was about five years ago; funny, we've all left but Brother Laurence." He pointed to one of the men in the photo. "He didn't know what to do on the outside. I was lucky because dad took me in," he said.

Jeff picked up the guitar and tuned it as he talked. He wasn't three feet from me, and I could feel his energy again, strong and sensual but unowned somehow, inadvertent. It seemed almost a danger to him, like the scent of a hare that draws the hound on its trail. I wondered suddenly if Jeff had been abused in the seminary like you hear about in the news.

We finished the coffee and headed back into the examination room. Jeff put Brutus on the table, took some skin scrapings and looked at them under the microscope. Mange was caused by a dog's reaction to mites, he explained. You diagnose mange by finding mites although it wasn't foolproof, since the reaction to mites could continue long after the mites themselves were gone. But Brutus's slide showed mites, many mites, so the diagnosis was clear.

Jeff cleaned out the crusted and scabby areas of the dog's skin, then applied some cream that smelled faintly of myrrh. He loaded me up with medicated shampoo, antibiotics and vitamin drops to add to Brutus's food and instructions to bring him back in two weeks. He absolutely refused to let me pay.

"It's for me more than anything else," he said, fingering the gold hoop in his ear and looking down. "I've made so many compromises along the way, in the seminary, then with dad. Helping this dog feels like I'm standing up for myself somehow, becoming real again."

Brutus healed quickly. His sores improved the next week, and the raw infected patches had transformed into hairless pink skin by the time I took him back for new skin scrapings. That visit, Jeff gave Brutus a distemper vaccine and a heartworm test. The following week he x-rayed the dog's ribs and front left leg. Two ribs had been broken and the leg had suffered a hairline twist fracture.

"Typical fighting wounds," he said, as he poured out coffee. "He was obviously matched against a bigger dog, but he's still alive, so that says something. Dad says it is a kind of natural selection, the strong, fit dogs live on to create a better species. Not that he condones dog fighting of course; no vet's ever going to do that. But he doesn't think we should get so emotional about it." Jeff made a face and smiled. "I'm working on it," he said.

There was a fight late one afternoon out in the dirt alley

behind Garden Court. I heard fight noises, the gasping for breath, the scuffling, the men shouting.

"It's the Mexicans fighting dogs again," Michael said.

It seemed brazen to hold a dog fight in the middle of a summer afternoon, but when I looked out the garbage bin opening in the fence, there they were, a half dozen men gathered round, whistling and shouting encouragement to the fighters. In the center was a dusty struggling mass. I stopped breathing and every detail of the scene came into sharp focus.

One man leaned close into the fight. He was short, shirtless, with a tattoo on his right arm. "No fear" it said. He did not see me. He was absorbed in the action.

"Go for the eyes, Buddy," he called to one of them. In that instant, I saw that he was not Mexican, none of them were Mexican. The fighters were not dogs, either, but boys, two boys maybe ten years old.

"The eyes, Buddy, then knee his balls," the tattooed man instructed. The boy on top stuffed his hand open over the other boy's face as he squirmed to break free.

I knew I had to do something, should do something, must do something, but I could not move. The violence seemed to paralyze me where I stood, while, just yards away, the top boy brought his knee hard into the other boy, and the men cheered at his gasp. I could not move or even breathe. Only my hands moved, trembling uncontrollably.

I heard heavy footfalls from behind me in Garden Court. Somebody was pushing from behind me, pushing past me. It was the veteran, but he seemed different, huge. He towered above the men. His shadow falling on the boys froze them into place, but the man coaching Buddy looked up angrily.

"Get lost," he said. "My kid, my property. I do what I want."

"Shut up before I shut you up," the veteran said, his voice so low you could barely hear it, yet I thought the quality of voice alone would knock them all over. It was the voice of someone fully prepared to kill. The men stared at him, moving away a little. The veteran faced off against the tattooed man, but the other dropped his eyes and backed away, scowling. Buddy dropped off the other boy too and the rest of the men stepped farther back. The veteran walked into the circle and offered his hand to the smaller boy. The boy did not take it though. He got up to a crouch, spit on the ground, then took off limping fast down the dirt alley. The veteran stood there for several seconds with his hand still extended. I could not take my eyes off his hand. It was trembling, just like my own. Finally, he turned and went back into Garden Court.

It seemed that summer would last forever in the little town as sunny days followed sunny days and new buds replaced wilting blooms on each azalea bush, surge after surge of sun and flowers that did not seem to draw down their sources, like ocean waves rise and fall and crash against the shore, splintering into a million drops without changing by one centimeter the level of the ocean. In the sunshine, with the help of medicine Jeff provided, the little dog's sores healed over completely, and black hair grew in, sparsely at first, then thicker and longer until his entire back was smooth fur. Jasmine foamed white over the Garden Court trellis, the scent powerful and confident, and new pink and yellow rosebuds appeared, bloomed and faded, making room for others to follow. Even the slender bush outside my kitchen window grew fat with new leaves. In time it offered up one white bud, facing in toward my kitchen as if to protect itself from passing eyes and hands. Summer still held court from sunrise to sunset; only the nights edged toward autumn as the ocean fog crept in more and more often to thicken the dark after midnight and the willow shed water almost every morning.

For a long time, I guarded the flowers and would not let anyone cut them, but there were always more and more and one day, when nobody was out, I took a small cutting of a bright red geranium. It had no powerful perfume like the roses or the jasmine, yet it smelled so strong of sunny days and cool wet nights that all my cabin filled with that and I almost felt I too would sprout leaves and grow.

One morning, early, I decided to walk to the woods to see the redwoods weeping. Instead of heading up to the cafe, I crossed the open field of the abandoned park, walked past the apple tree to enter the dark of the forest. I was resolved to go as deep in as I had to, but I did not have to go very far. Even as I stepped from sunny field to shadow, I heard a gentle tapping of drops on earth and felt the water on my skin. I walked a dozen steps then was stopped still in the cool quiet of the forest: redwoods, tall and grave, stood all around me, oblivious to my presence, weeping, weeping, some deep sorrow. I shut my eyes and felt the water on my cheeks and, from somewhere else, I watched the individual droplets run down the plane of my face, like rain on a window can be seen from either side.

I asked Shae what she knew about the altar back in the forest. She had been there once, she said, to an AA picnic some years back. She said it was supposed to be haunted. Years ago, she said, the stump that made up the altar was a really tall tree. Some men got the bright idea to cut it down and take it on tour around the country, but when they felled it, it crushed them. She said the place had served as a church for a time, then as a lovers' lane for local kids until weird things started happening.

"So, who haunts it?" Michael asked. "The men or the tree?"

Shae wasn't sure but she said she would ask at the meeting that night and the next day she said nobody knew but it happened when there was a full moon.

The next time I went to the library, I brought back a booklet on the redwood preserve. I carried it out to the picnic table at lunchtime and read the interesting parts aloud.

The redwood grove was discovered in the 1800's when a man hunting deer came upon the tallest tree he had ever seen, twice as tall as any tree around it. He showed it to friends, and they told other people about it. It came to the attention of German speculators who decided to take it on tour around the country. They chopped it down with augers and wedges since no saws were big enough. It took five men twenty-two days to drill all the holes, the book said, but the tree was perfectly symmetrical and it did not fall for a week.

"So, what about the ghosts?" Michael asked. He was eating reheated frozen fish fingers from his yellow lunch plate. He could only eat four of them at a sitting, but he always cooked five fingers at a time as if it were some sort of a rule.

The book did not say anything about ghosts. It did say that two German nationals were killed when the tree fell, and it said the men stripped the bark off the tree to take on tour around the country, that the reconstructed tree trunk had been lost in an avalanche as they took it across the Rockies, and it listed other facts about the trees themselves. It said that redwood bark is fire-resistant, but that fire does sometimes manage to burn through and carve out a chamber inside the still living tree. When this happens, a thin layer of sapwood grows over the burn scar. The sapwood transports the water and nutrients that keep the hollow tree alive.

Michael frowned at this and told Larry to set up the checkerboard, but Larry was listening carefully. When I finished reading about the sapwood, he walked over to inspect the two redwood trees between my cabin and the empty one. He said he could not see any sapwood on them, but there were flat lumps on one trunk, like little shelves. The book told about those too: they were called "burls," and the tree grew them to keep its balance when some outside force caused it to lean to one side. Larry wrote the words "sapwood" and "burls" on two little slips of paper and tucked them into his wallet. When Michael asked why he kept the words, Larry said that the sapwood was for himself, the burls for his brother Harry.

It was a couple of days later when Tina showed up in Garden Court. We were all sitting outside finishing up lunch when she walked under the entryway trellis right over to the picnic table. Her hair was still in a messy ponytail, but she looked different. Her right eye was swollen and both front teeth were broken. She rolled up the sleeves of her muumuu to show us the bruises on her arms. She said that Johnny got drunk and hit her around the night before. When she came to it was afternoon and he was still passed out, so she came over to see Shae. Shae let her take a shower, then pulled out the numbers for the battered women's shelters in the area.

"He went to jail for it last time," Tina told us. "I swore I'd never see the bastard again." She lit a cigarette and blew out the smoke. Shae lit one too.

"Call the cops," Shae barked.

"He got out of jail and come over and I wasn't doing nothing so we went out a couple times and he moved in."

"Call the cops," Shae repeated. "Even if you love him, you have to stand up for yourself."

"Love that bastard?" Tina said. "That would smack a girl because she didn't get him a drink fast enough? That would sic his pit on a little collie passing by? I'd like to see him dead."

Shae told Tina that there was an empty cabin in Garden Court and that if she wanted to move in, we would put in a good word to management for her. Tina thought something might be wrong with the cabin if nobody rented it. I popped the door lock with my credit card, and we all walked through; it looked okay, even Tina agreed. She drank the coffee Shae gave her and smoked the cigarette, then she stood up to go.

"Now, what is your plan?" Shae asked.

"Well," said Tina. "I guess I'll just go see he's okay." Shae blew smoke into the air and rolled her eyes.

After Tina left, I headed over to the abandoned park to talk to old Michael. It was safer to talk to him in the mornings because he allowed himself only one beer before noon and he was often alone. But that afternoon, Michael was alone except for Mollybelle, and he did not seem too drunk. I told him about Tina and asked if she was crazy.

He shrugged. "Few are really lunatic," he said, "that's my belief. Few really touched by the moon. Most of us just circle round and round some bleeding core, some wound we can't see and deny exists."

I remembered the amphitheater then and asked what he knew about the altar back in the redwoods. He said that he had been out to the old church once when the moon was full, some years back, with a sharp loneliness biting at his heart. Those days, the darkness was always with him. He had sat down in one of the benches, looked at the stump and had a few nips of whiskey. When he looked up again, he saw the whole tree rising from the altar like a tall shining cloud, the ghost of the tree towering above everything.

"Then, lass, a funny thing happened," Michael said. "I began to weep, old drunk that I am, me as had never shed a tear, weeping for my mam, dead fifty year. Her scent came to me suddenly, and I remembered her holding me as a lad before she died, and I wept as she was dead and I'd never mourned her before."

I resolved at that moment to walk back and look for the ghost tree by moonlight. I tried to talk the others into going with me, but Michael and Larry were afraid of the dark and Shae had her meeting every evening. Then one night the electricity in town went off so Shae's meeting was shorter than usual, and we decided to go. Shae helped Larry light up candles, and we left Brutus with him for protection, then she and I set off with flashlights. The moon was not quite full but almost. We talked and joked a little as we walked across the open field but after we entered the redwood forest, it was too quiet to talk. I walked first because my neon green flashlight was stronger, and I shone the light from side to side to make sure nobody was hiding in the brush. I could hear Shae's footsteps close behind me.

We followed the path up, up, to the crest of the hill. I warned Shae about the statue to the left of the path and when we got to the crest of the hill, I shown my light over to it. We stepped off the path and stopped in front of the statue to inspect it. The hooded head still looked too small for the body, as if the sculptor had forgotten he had to make a hood until the last minute, then carved it out of the head itself. The small triangular face with slits for eyes looked evil in the moonlight.

"I hope it's not him that haunts the place," Shae said. She laughed but her voice and the laugh sounded small and brittle in the thickness of the night. We stood there silently, looking at the statue and listening to the silence, and after a time I turned my light back to the path. But before I took a step, twigs cracked from up the path in the direction from which we had come. I snapped off my light and Shae did the same and we jumped behind the base of the statue and crouched down. We heard footsteps tracing our footsteps and male voices, then two dark figures appeared, passing not ten feet away. I was sure they would see us, and my heart was booming loud enough to vibrate every redwood branch in the area. My body started shaking and my teeth tried to clack together like a skeleton, but the dark forms passed by and disappeared over the crest of the hill.

Shae and I burst from behind the statue and ran back down the hill toward the town. Again, I felt that sense of déjà vu and I ran to save my life, my heart sounding like a chiming clock in the worthless body, and Shae ran too, as fast as she could go. She fell once but leaped back up and later I ran into a tree branch and dropped my flashlight, but we kept moving and before long we saw the open park and the familiar apple tree. We stopped to rest because Shae was limping from her fall and I wrapped my arms around that tree to ground me. We calmed down and began to laugh a little, then more and more until we were laughing there like fools, but I did not go back for the flashlight.

The lights of the town were still out. When we got back to Garden Court, Robbie and George were sitting with Larry and the dog on the deck. We snuck in the garbage way and said "Boo!" and they jumped and Robbie shrieked and Brutus started barking and everything seemed pretty funny. Shae made instant coffee on Larry's camping stove and served it up in her mum's five-thousand-dollar silver tea set, and Michael brought out some chips and a snack for the dog.

I carried pillows out to the deck, and everyone sat

around in the warm night air. By the light of the moon and the plumbers' candles, we filled Robbie and George in on the ghost stories and the booklet from the library and on the other stories we had heard. Shae told again about heading for the amphitheater and how we lost the flashlight, making it funnier this time and everyone laughed and laughed.

"So, were they the ghosts?" Larry asked, after we'd gone through it a couple of times, as though he may have missed the most important part of the story.

"Well, if they were, somebody got the story wrong," Shae said. "These ghosts were speaking perfect English."

George had his arm around Robbie and Shae ruffled Larry's hair and mixed Michael more coffee. Michael started telling about how, if you shine a flashlight into the sky, the beam travels on for light-years like a signal to other planets of where you were even if you were not there anymore. Everybody listened and then told other stories and the scent of the jasmine blew across us, flickering the candle flames, and I felt wave after wave of well-being wash upon my eroded shore. The smell of summer encircled us, seeming almost to come from the candle flames themselves, and the moon was overhead like some huge, natural candle not affected by the winds of earth, some welcome beam signaling us from far away. The dog crept over and leaned into me, his eyes wide and expressionless in the candlelight, and I whispered to him not to be afraid, that he was not all alone any more, that he had friends now, that nobody would ever be able to hurt him again.

CHAPTER 12

THERE WAS A moment on the river when summer held us in her pause. Then it passed, collapsing in, onto itself, falling softly but irrevocably like petals off a rose.

As summer moved on, the days crisped around the edges, beginning later and ending earlier. Cool breezes pushed the tourists from the river beach, swept the leaves from the trees. I would often wear a light jacket when I walked up to the cafe in the early mornings, and sometimes the streetlights would still glow faintly, offering a muffled warning that the days of warmth and light were fading. By five-thirty in the afternoon, the sun dipped behind the redwoods and we stayed in Garden Court.

One Thursday afternoon, Larry went in for his appointment with the county psychiatrist. The psychiatrist kept office hours in the Mental Health Center every Monday and Thursday and everyone on government disability on the River had to pass through his doors at least twice a year to continue to receive the stipend. So many River people qualified for SSI that the doctor did not spend very long with any of them; Shae joked that his main job was to verify that the people getting checks were still alive. Larry was back after fifteen minutes.

A week or so after the appointment, Shae told me she thought Larry had started the meds again. She guessed that the shrink had given him the same prescriptions and that Larry was hiding the bottles in his van. She outlined the evidence: Larry stopped by his old, broken-down van several times a day now for no apparent reason, a new habit. He woke up later and later in the morning and rarely felt like doing anything except watching television. He'd even turned down a fishing trip with George and Robbie. Shae said she was going to leave him if he'd started up again. Meds were meds, even if a shrink prescribed them, and she could not go on like this. In the past, each time the shrink gave Larry a two-month supply of meds, he ended up overdosing and the dance began again.

All I knew was that Larry came out to the picnic table less often, but summer was passing and the late afternoon sunshine no longer welcomed us like a friend. An uneasiness began to creep back in as well, like the refrain of a symphony wending its slow way back to the surface. I told myself that things would go on as they were, but our world was changing, the darkness creeping in, extending long, thin fingers into Garden Court. The nightmares returned. One night I dreamed I was one of a handful of children kidnapped by men wearing white hoods. We huddled in the dark near a bonfire, waiting to hear which of us would be chosen to die. I woke up trembling, every inch of my body icy cold except for the back of my legs where Brutus lay pressed against me.

My duties as groundskeeper changed as summer waned. I raked up fallen leaves, cut back the bushes where flowers were wilting, but the wild burst of new colors, the exuberant race of green magic up dead stalks, was over. Nature was slowing down, packing up for the winter.

Brutus had recovered remarkably well, his fur thick and rich, his muscles strong and well-defined. Jeff wanted to do periodic skin scrapings until he was sure the mite infection had cleared, so I continued to take him up every few weeks. I never made an appointment. If Jeff was in with a client, I waited in the entry room, Brutus beneath my chair.

Once, as I sat there waiting, the outside door opened and a man walked in. He was a tall man of late middle age, respectable, a solid citizen in working man's khakis and an old fighter-pilot jacket like my dad used to wear. He had big hands, big arms, everything about him seemed big, but not giant or grotesque. Simply a big man, a man's man who knew how to use a gun and land a fish and take care of himself in a fight. But he did not have the look of a fighter, his face was too genial, brown eyes pleasant, nose stocky, lips full. His head was bald, and what was left on the sides was gray, cut very short. Maybe it was his gray hair or maybe it was his jaw, set and stern, but something about him made me think of steel. Yet he smiled when he saw me there in the waiting room, smiled and walked over.

"My son's running late, is he?" he said.

I started to explain that I was waiting for the vet, but just then Jeff walked out. His face lit up. "Hey Dad," he said, hurrying over to shake his hand. "Great to see you. How are those pigs coming?"

The man was half a head taller than Jeff, and he looked down at him affectionately. "Finished testing this morning, worked all night since Butch is slaughtering tomorrow," he said. "I was heading out to hit some balls, thought I'd stop by, see how things are going."

Jeff's eyes shot to the desk, cluttered with loose papers and odds and ends, then he let his glance drift to the examination room behind as if to hide the initial gesture. His father looked toward the exam room as well.

"Go right ahead," he told Jeff, nodding his approval. "You never want to keep a client waiting, especially such a pretty one. The owner, I mean, not the pet," he said, and winked at me. "I was so busy admiring this lovely lady that I forgot to look for her pet, but it can't be far behind."

Brutus lay motionless under my chair. When I rose to my feet, he came out to stand by my side. Jeff's father gave a laugh and was saying, "I knew this young lady did not come in alone," but the end of his sentence trailed off. The man was staring hard at Brutus. After a minute, he caught himself and laughed again. "On the other hand," he said, "I did not expect a pit bull."

Jeff chuckled with his dad, then turned to me to explain. "Don't take it as a criticism," he said. "Dad's old-school, prefers pit bulls to poodles. Don't you Dad?"

His father snorted. "There you are right, son," he said. "When I learned to be a vet, we treated bulls not parakeets. The only dogs we saw were working dogs."

Jeff bloomed under this approval. He stood up a little

taller and moved closer to the man as if hoping to hold his attention. "You should have seen this dog when she first brought him in, Dad," Jeff told him. "Bad case of mange, secondary infection, the dog so thin you could count his ribs. Look at him now." He squatted down and Brutus went straight to him, pushing his muzzle against his knees. Jeff scratched the dog's ears, but his eager eyes never left his father's face.

The older man's gaze returned to Brutus. He looked at him intently again, greedily, for many minutes. The air in the room thickened, making it hard to breathe.

"Doesn't he look good Dad?" Jeff said finally.

"He sure does," the man said quickly, nodding several times and picking something out of a back tooth with his thumbnail. "Sorry about staring, it's just that he looks a little like a dog old Curley used to keep on the Helm ranch. But don't let me hold you up. Another day, another dollar. We'll talk afterward."

He took off his coat and settled himself at the desk while I followed Jeff into the exam room. As Jeff lifted Brutus onto the exam table to get the scrapings, I tried to catch his eye, but he did not look at me. He seemed nervous and kept biting his lip. The first slide he made up fell and shattered on the tile floor and he had to start again.

Finally, the procedure was over. For the first time, the slide showed no mites. Brutus seemed to understand, and he leaped off the table, jumping around and wagging his tail like a puppy, but Jeff paid scant attention. His eyes kept flicking toward the front room where his dad sat at the desk flipping through mail. The pause grew uncomfortable.

"So, what do I owe you?" I said.

Jeff did not meet my eyes. It was a moment before he spoke. "That'll be twenty dollars," he said, his voice cracking like an adolescent.

It was about that time that I started taking Brutus with me to the cafe in the mornings. Dogs were not allowed in the cafe so I would tie him outside, near the window where I could keep my eye on him. Even when I read the newspaper, a part of me remained infinitely aware of the dog and nobody could pass without being picked up in my radar. One day I looked up in panic, but it was only Shae, patting the dog's round head.

It seemed early for Shae to be up and about, but then I remembered that she had booked an eight o'clock appointment with Larry's psychiatrist. The only time slots available had been early morning or after Christmas so she had made the effort.

Shae walked in, bought a coffee, and slammed it down on my table. Half of the coffee slurped out, but she did not notice.

"That shrink won't tell me anything about Larry's treatment," she said in a loud, shrill voice. "Nothing! I told him stuff he needed to know, like how Larry's dad tried to shoot Larry but the bullet ricocheted and killed him instead; how Harry blamed Larry for their dad's death and tried to kill Larry too; how Larry uses those meds to get away from the pain and so many at once are too much for him to resist.

"But he cut me off! Said I needed counseling myself if I couldn't see that Larry's treatment was none of my business." Shae gulped some of the coffee from her mug, looking in surprise for a moment at the small amount that remained, before rushing on.

"I said that, as someone who has driven Larry to the hospital four times to have those meds pumped out of his stomach, I had somewhat of an interest. I told him that if he continued prescribing psychotropic meds in two-month quantities, he had better increase his malpractice insurance because I was not going to take another suicide lying down. He laughed right in my face and said that wasn't much of a threat, that I couldn't even bring a lawsuit about Larry's treatment because I wasn't married to him!"

Shae talked for a long time, all through her free refill, sometimes curling her tongue out and up as if it helped her to keep her thoughts coming. But after a while she sped off to an appointment with her disability hearing lawyer. She had to keep a close eye on him too, she said, since a friend had seen him playing golf with her doctor just last week.

When I went back to Garden Court, Larry sat alone at the picnic table. It had been a week or so since I'd seen him out there, so I sat with him, Brutus at our feet. Larry had so much sorrow in his life, yet he never spoke of it. That morning he seemed ready to talk but not about his life. Instead, he asked casually where the weeds came from. The big weeds seemed to have laid low all summer to appear in force at the end of the season, just where I had worked the soil. It looked like someone had spread weed seeds when I was not looking.

I pulled out the book on plants to see if it might say something about it. In fact, there was an entire section on weeds. It said that weed seeds lie dormant below the surface of the soil for years and years until some unsuspecting gardener tills them to the surface and they spring to life.

"So, it's your fault," Larry said mildly, like a joke.

"I guess so," I said. I thought about all the digging I had done trying to clean things up. How ironic it would be if I had unleashed the very thing I had been trying to eliminate. It wouldn't be the first time. I thought of the panic attacks, how everything got worse when I'd focused on them. Eventually Larry went inside to watch television, but I stayed outside with Brutus.

After a while, Shae came back from her meeting with the news: Her lawyer denied playing golf at all, much less with her doctor, so that had been a false alarm. She had picked up an extra copy of the big city newspaper and handed it over to me, then she went in to make us coffee. It was getting chilly. When Shae came out with coffee, she brought a blanket and spread it over Brutus who was lying on the ground at my feet. He stood up underneath it and turned around and around until he was twisted up inside the blanket, then he flopped down with his back pressed against my foot and fell asleep.

Shae and I sat and drank the coffee. Then she brought out the law book I'd lent her and asked me to clear up a few points her lawyer had not explained to her satisfaction. But she stopped in the middle of a question and asked: "Who's the little girl crying?"

I glanced around Garden Court for a child, maybe the cooking lady's daughter, but Shae held up a photo that had been tucked into the text like a bookmark, the same one I came across when Jack knocked books to the floor in my back room: a child looking out of a white-cased window, her front teeth missing.

"Crying?" I said. "I'm not crying."

"It's you?" she asked.

When Shae went in to get us more coffee, I picked up the little photo and looked at it carefully: the dark curls, the lines of the face precise as a new leaf. I peered at the eyes; they were full of tears. I'd never noticed before. My stomach felt empty and churning. I replaced the photo in the book before Shae came back to the table and we talked about other things.

Just as the sun dipped behind the trees, a man walked up the footpath. I knew that taut, rough energy: It was Johnny, Tina's boyfriend. Tina was not with him. Neither Shae nor I said hello, but he walked over anyway.

"I decided to take the dog," he told us. I felt Brutus push against me a little harder and I willed him to keep still.

"How's Tina?" Shae asked him.

He looked at her hard for a minute. The last time he could not meet her eyes at all but this time he did. He held them for a minute as if he were going to say something but then decided not to, just made a gesture with his head and shoulders saying okay, she was okay.

"I decided to take that dog, Brutus," he told us again.

"Too late," Shae said. "He's not up for grabs anymore. Anyway, word is you got a big pit of your own."

The man thought this one through silently, leaning his body a bit more forward than its natural tilt. Then he asked Shae who got him.

"He's not available anymore so what's it to you?" she said, lighting a cigarette and puffing smoke out the side of her mouth as she talked.

"Maybe they'll sell him," Johnny shrugged. "Worth a try."

"So why do you want him suddenly?" Shae asked. "He hasn't grown any."

"You know what they say," Johnny said. "Size ain't everything. I hear he's real game."

"What do you mean by that?" Shae said, scowling.

"He don't quit," Johnny said. Now that he had Shae's attention, he took his time, pulling out his pack, lighting up a cigarette, before he continued. "I hear from a guy that knows. That dog goes on and on and no matter what, he don't quit, absorbs punishment like a sponge. A deep game dog like you don't find real often. So whoever got him, I want to talk."

Shae said to forget it, he would not get the dog if he was the last person on earth, but Johnny walked over to the table and stood right next to me. I did not hear Brutus growl, but I could feel his body growling low, low.

"So, where's the dog, girly?" he asked me, leaning over me. "I got a real deal dogman telling me he's a roller. I think I'll just wait around and see if that dog don't come back." I felt my body tremble and found I couldn't speak, but Shae told him to get lost and if he ever touched Tina again, she would call the cops even if Tina did not, so he left. I unwound Brutus from the blanket and moved him into the cabin and locked the doors.

I was sitting at my kitchen table with the newspaper a few hours later when a scream from up the footpath rang through Garden Court. I was reading an article about a five-year-old girl who had died. Her stepfather would test her on the alphabet, making her say it very fast. If she made a single slip, he had her fill up the bathtub and then he would hold her head under water as punishment. The last time he told her to fill up the tub, she clung to her mother sobbing and crying but finally she had to do it. The man held her under too long that time and she died. "A kid's only job is to obey," he explained to the policeman. "First commandment: honor thy father."

I was reading that report, feeling dizzy from it but unable to put it down, when I heard the scream from up the footpath. It did not sound like the scream of an adult woman but a child's scream, high and breathless and I raced outside, my heart pounding, Brutus behind me. We weren't the only ones. Shae rushed out onto the deck and the veteran strode out of his cabin with a baseball bat and his pistol. Down the footpath ran Felicia, screaming and screaming until she collapsed on Shae's steps. The whole scene could have manifested directly from my own nightmares.

There was nobody running behind Felicia, no blood pouring down her body, so everyone gathered round to hear what had happened. Even Michael ventured out. Felicia caught her breath, then she began talking in Spanish. I understood enough Spanish to make out that the devil was in her house, *el diablo*. She could say no more.

The veteran said to get a flashlight, so I found the one I'd bought to replace the green one I dropped in the woods, and we all trooped to Felicia's cabin together. The veteran prepared to bust in the door, but Felicia pointed up, above the door, to a spot near the roof. I directed the beam up that way. I saw a hole, but not a very large one. Nobody could see anything in the hole at first, then suddenly we saw it, a small furry animal with a face like a little bear. You could see the hooks on its elbows and the flaps of skin extending from the arms to the feet.

Shae snorted. "It's just a bat," she said with disgust. "You are afraid of a bat?"

Suddenly the bat launched itself out of the attic, heading straight at us. Everyone shrieked and ran, even the veteran, and I could hear the high-pitched scream of the bat, and then other bats following it, their turns sharp as they angled off into the night.

We stopped running down by Shae's and laughed and laughed, and Michael did a really good imitation of Shae saying "You are afraid of a bat?" just before she took off running herself, and we laughed until we fell down. Shae explained things to Larry and Vama, and they laughed too, but Shae and Michael and I laughed hysterically, as if our lives had been in danger and suddenly were not.

Felicia did not laugh at all, however. She sat down on the deck stairs, her face stern and pale. "Una signa mala," she repeated to herself, as if nobody else were there and she was all alone in a situation out of control. "Una signa muy mala."

Shae told her to report the bats to management the next morning, and we expected her to tack a few crosses to the door and let it pass, but Felicia packed up that very night and moved out of Garden Court without a word to any of us. She left the cabin doors and windows wide open and management did not bother to shut them for a week. Each time you went by the empty cabin, you felt a chill.

"A bad sign," Larry repeated mournfully, whenever anyone mentioned Felicia.

Shae was having none of it. "Hah," she said. "Her and her bad signs. Didn't it seem like a bad sign when her only daughter went and moved in with the town mortician?"

CHAPTER 13

WHEN FALL CAME, it came quickly. One day the leaves shone a deep, vibrant green, the next they were flushed with yellow as if they had been burned by some inner fire. Yellow turned to orange, then to red, and when the leaves began to fall, no force on earth was powerful enough to stop them.

Autumn brought its own colors, but they were the colors of endings, the dirty browns of dead and dying leaves, fading flowers, needles that had taken the last, long fall. Gone was the sense that God surged through every blade of grass. Most of the grasses and flowers withered back and Garden Court looked empty and abandoned once again. It was as if something strong and good had come onto the river, protecting us by its very presence, and one morning, we woke to find it gone. Fear seeped into the empty spaces it left behind, multiplying like bacteria, growing stronger in the damp darkness.

I sat in the cafe and watched a fierce wind blow by. It pushed clouds in from the ocean, dark-edged clouds, not the fluffy white scooters of spring but heavy clouds with jagged stringy edges like pelt that blew across the bland, careless face of the autumn sky. Old Michael trudged by the cafe in his long coat with the wind behind him, his eyes worried and withdrawn, and it looked like he and Mollybelle were pushed along just like the fallen leaves. Mickey and Lulabelle blew by next, Lulabelle well in front, and one of the cops in the cafe joked about whether to call them the tramps with dogs or the dogs with tramps.

"Still," said the other cop, "since the day those two hooked up with the dogs, we haven't had a day of trouble with them. We ought to get Bear and company some mutts too."

The last of the summer people left the little town one weekend in early autumn, a three-day weekend for those who worked, of whom there were not many on the river. Shae said the summer people might come back for a few more Saturdays if the weather was nice, then that was it for the year. Many of the houses and cabins were already closed up, windows shuttered, like eyes shut tight against what lay ahead.

With the exodus of the summer people, those of us who remained saw more of each other, like it or not. I ran into the men living in the condemned apartments, for example, whenever I left Garden Court. They had little work now and wandered the empty streets more openly, and in the late afternoons they went to the abandoned park. Old Michael still reigned in the mornings, but in the hours before twilight, the bench under the apple tree was occupied by groups of young men and their dogs.

The strange men in the park seemed a bad omen to me, and I stopped walking that direction in the evenings. I had no legal claim to either the park or old Michael, but both had become fixtures in the structure of my small, new life and I felt threatened by their loss. As summer collapsed around my shoulders, the dank claustrophobic dread returned each morning, the sense of entrapment without hope of escape.

With the autumn came the rains, weeks of rain predicted and talk of renewed flooding to come. When the ground is saturated, any rainfall will cause flooding, the newspaper said. Shae scoffed at this, but the river was rising. On the way back from Safeway one evening, I headed over to the bridge near Johnson's Beach to check the watermark. I'd left Brutus back in my cabin, and I was alone, the streets deserted. It was not late, but the embers of the sunset had already died out, and everything was shades of gray, the beach ashen, the metal bridge dark as charred wood.

I walked the narrow bridge out to mid-span, then stood for a time looking over the railing, watching steel-gray water flow west toward the sea. The surface of the river was not broken by waves; there was only the rise and fall of deep ripples, like muscles flexing under skin. The empty beach was eerie, devoid of life, even the memory of life. The crowds of happy summer people, the hundred sunny summer days, had left no trace. Gone, all gone.

The cold crept inside me awakening a deeper cold within, a deadness at the very heart. I heard the familiar melody; it had only seemed to pass, now it was back, rising from the ashes of the summer, the old refrain of darkness and of death. I was empty and dirty with this craziness rising inside me; a pretty package filled with rot that seeped slowly through the seams of the shell I had constructed. I was bone-weary of the fight to contain it.

I looked down at the churning water. If I fell, it would be cold for a moment, then not, passing smoothly from emptiness to emptiness, almost a coming home. The word *home* brought tears, but I pushed them back. Do it this time and be done. The top of the railing was cold hard metal. I found a foothold, swung a leg over the top, then the other until I stood on the outside of the railing, leaning over into darkness.

Is it time, now? May I go now from these barren fields? No need to jump, just let go and fall, the body turning a little, hitting the water about there, I could just see the spot in the deepening dusk, the river rolling. Then, as I looked, my eye caught a different movement in the water, something cutting cross-current, breaking the surface just a little, moving toward the silent beach. Terror gripped me, that forever fear, stronger than the cold, and I watched, heart pounding for my age-old enemy to emerge and make himself known.

At length, a form appeared on the beach from the darkness of the river. I knew that form, that shape, although I had not seen it for months. The layered muscles and small cruel eyes. It was the shadow dog, dark and heartless. I stood still, not moving so much as a finger, not breathing, yet prey can never hide from a predator long and the dog immediately sensed my presence. It turned toward the bridge, holding its gaze even as it shook river water from its body, raising its muzzle to catch the scent. After a moment, the dog disappeared into the undergrowth beside Johnson's Beach.

I stood there for a time unable to move my eyes from the beach where the shadow dog had been, then the spell broke. The urge toward death was still with me, but the current of fear swept me back toward Brutus; Brutus waiting for me back in the cabin. If I did not return, he would surely meet with sorrow, surely fall into Johnny's hands. An image came to me of Johnny holding Brutus on a lead as the shadow dog lunged toward him. I saw Brutus's eyes, dark and wide, and they seemed to be filled with tears.

I swung my leg over the railing, pulled myself over, and hurried back to River Road. I had to save Brutus. He had nobody but me to stand up for him. I would not let them get him. I was running now, and my footsteps on the wet pavement beat hollow and lonely in the silence of the empty streets. A chill wind pushed me up the Garden Court footpath to my cabin. I unlocked the door and pushed it open. Brutus sat in the corner, ears pulled back as if he were preparing for a fight. And then he leaped toward me, bounding like a lamb, his body pushing eagerly against my legs. Brutus, my boy Brutus. I knelt down and wrapped my arms around him. It was at that moment that the truth came to me: It was Brutus who had saved me. The idea of my saving Brutus was just rhetoric, cold words and empty logic. It was love of the dog Brutus that had saved my life.

CHAPTER 14

ALTHOUGH THE LITTLE town emptied out at the close of summer, nobody moved from Garden Court. Instead, a new person moved in. A boy named Tony rented the empty cabin on the other side of my cabin. Tony was neither tall nor short, just about normal, and he had styled, medium brown hair, a light tan and a quick, energetic manner. He moved in one afternoon with the help of two male friends and three girls, all in new jeans and clean T-shirts. It felt like an invasion.

I kept working in the garden and Larry and Michael tried to play checkers as usual, but the newcomer's chatty energy bounced strangely through the entire court. Even Vama came out, dishcloth over her shoulder to tell Tony and his friends to shut up, although they were not being particularly loud. Tony replied courteously to Vama, and later he walked over to the picnic table. He shook hands all round and said he was stocking shelves at Safeway for the fall because he had applied too late for the community college. Tony wore brand new Nikes and had styled hair, but he patted the dog and greeted Larry's cat without making any jokes about the missing eye or ear, so it was hard to justify disliking him.

When Tony told us his plans and introduced himself, Michael spoke up. He pointed at me and said I was a famous lawyer just vacationing on the River and that his brother was a lawyer too. Tony just smiled, showing white, even teeth, and said that he would not hold it against us, and I had a feeling that something had ended and that the end had begun.

I told Shae that Tony seemed too normal to belong in Garden Court. She had that same feeling, but said she'd thought that about me too at first. And, as time passed, we got used to Tony. He worked long hours, so we did not often see him around and, when we did, he always had something pleasant to say, so we went on as we were for a time.

One by one, the plants of Garden Court died back. Although I knew it was nature's cycle, something inside of me was frantic to help them, to heal them, to save them from their fate. After the raking and the mulching, there was nothing I could do, so I spent more time with Brutus. Most mornings I took him to the abandoned park to let him run with Mollybelle and Lulabelle while I sat with old Michael and Mickey.

Once I arrived too late and the bench beneath the old tree was empty. Brutus looked up at me, wagging his tail, eyes shining. I didn't have the tennis ball, but the ground was strewn with hard, green apples, so I picked one up and threw it as far as I could. Brutus leaped after it in a second, speeding down the footpath, sweeping up the apple without pausing an instant. He circled back triumphantly to lay it like an offering at my feet. I threw it again and again. After a half-dozen tosses, the apple got mushy, so I picked up another one and threw it, then another. Brutus never stopped moving, racing and bounding in the autumn air. After that we played apples every day.

As we were playing apples one day, Brutus stopped cold in his tracks, staring past me, up the rise. Every muscle of his body hardened at the same moment, as if an invisible wizard had turned the dog into stone. Adrenaline flooded my veins and I swung around, without even knowing I was doing it, pivoted to face the dirt alley. A dog stood there looking down at us, a rust-colored pit bull. It began approaching slowly, dragging a chain from its collar. The dog was built like a tractor, body low and powerful on muscular legs, and its ears were clipped close to his huge skull. It did not glance at me; its eyes were trained on Brutus.

Cold flooded my head, racing through my arms. The dog approached silently, not running but fast, stiff-legged. I threw my apple, hitting the dog squarely on the side of the head, but it did not so much as look in my direction. I stomped on the ground, yelled, screamed at Brutus to come to me, at the dog to go away. It was as if I did not exist. Brutus stood still, steady, ears back, trembling slightly, while the red pit closed in.

I looked around frantically for a weapon but found only apples, apples everywhere. I seized them up, charged toward the dog with my hands full of apples, but suddenly it lunged, and in that instant, they were fighting, the dogs were fighting, rolling over and over. All I saw were teeth, jaws, first one dog on top and then the other, snarling heads rising like flames in a roaring fire, descending to rise again. The rust-colored dog backed off, but it was only to go for a better hold, and over he went, as fast as lightening, but Brutus was faster. The other dog rolled, then Brutus rolled, and for a moment Brutus was on top, pinning the other dog by the throat.

I heard a horrible, high shriek that went on and on, then realized it was my own, but I could not stop it. I stood over the dogs, arms full of apples, screaming, the sound small and shrill in the open field. Suddenly, from behind me, boys streamed down from the alley, three of them, teenagers, white.

"Get out, lady, that dog will kill you," the first boy yelled, pushing me back. He grabbed the chain segment that was attached to the dog's collar, jerked it, then jerked it again, then the others were there too, working to break them up, to separate them, yelling at each other, at the dogs. Then someone shouted, "He's down!" or maybe "He's done." I ran back in, apples spilling from my arms like tears.

The boys huddled round the dogs, and I clawed through them, knocking one to the ground. There was blood and dog and more blood. Then there was Brutus. I threw my arms around him, lifted him up like a little child. He was alive, alive, warm in my arms. The boys remained silent. After a time, I looked down. The rust-colored dog lay on the ground under the apple tree in a dark pool. As it breathed, blood gurgled in and out through its sinuses. I turned to the boys, looked from one face to another, defying them to say a single word against my dog. Nobody said anything for a long moment. Finally, one boy spoke.

"How much you want for that pit, lady?" he said.

I carried Brutus to the vet clinic. The front room was empty, the door to the exam room open. I pushed through, and finally found Jeff in the den, sitting on the futon strumming his guitar. He leaped up when he saw me and took Brutus from my arms. He began an examination even before I was done explaining what had happened, bending each joint carefully, feeling along the back, the neck, talking softly to the dog, reassuring him. At last he looked up, raising his eyebrows and shaking his head, no major damage.

He cleaned and disinfected the wounds, then placed Brutus on the futon and poured me a cup of coffee. I had enough adrenaline in my veins that I could have gone without caffeine for a week, but I took the cup, felt its warmth against my chest. Jeff stood close to me, so close I could feel his warmth too.

"Listen, about the other day," he said.

I shook my head, dismissing it.

"Dad's kind of a hero to me," Jeff continued, looking down at his own coffee and talking low. "He's all work ethic, early to bed sort of thing, but you've got to realize that he came up from nothing. And he's done well for himself, bought up River properties when nobody wanted them, built up his practice." He paused again, and looking down at the clouds in his coffee, eyes far away. When he spoke again, his voice was even lower, and I had to lean close to him to hear.

"He saved me when I wanted to leave the Salesians.

Loaned me money for vet school, gave me a job. I don't see eye to eye with him on everything. But he's family. I owe him."

I nodded and drank my coffee, felt the caffeine zipping about in my veins. Jeff's arm was touching mine and the physical energy looped like electromagnetic fields, linking us, drawing us closer. I looked over at his face and he was looking at me, his eyes clear and kind. Just as he moved toward me, the phone rang, loud and shrill. Jeff leaped to his feet guiltily, still grasping his coffee. As he grabbed at the phone, he dropped the coffee cup and it plummeted to the floor, landing upright and spattering coffee everywhere, across my shoes, pants, across his. Brutus jumped off the couch barking.

"Hello," Jeff managed into the receiver. "Bordeaux Vet Clinic." It was a wrong number. In a minute he hung up the phone and reached for a roll of paper towels.

"Sorry," he said, sheepishly, shrugging. "I thought it was Dad."

I collected Brutus and took him home. We walked past the abandoned park, but it was empty; the boys and the dog were gone.

The following day, I instituted The Stick Policy. I found a solid stick that looked like it had been the handle of a rake or a shovel and I carried it out with me like a staff. I never took Brutus for a walk without it. But when little Michael saw it, he scoffed. A big dog would not even feel a stick like that, he said. Then I got the tire iron from my car, a metal rod bent slightly at the tip, and I carried that instead.

I slipped the straight end through a belt loop in my jeans and it hung from the bent tip like a sword. I took it every time I went out.

Most people did not notice the tire iron, but the Mexican men in the park did. I nodded politely and sternly to them to communicate that the tire iron had nothing to do with them, but this seemed to reinforce their impression that I was issuing a challenge. Once as I passed the park, the man sitting on the bench picked up a long, curved knife and began sharpening it slowly on a whetstone, never taking his eyes off my face. It occurred to me that I was creating danger for myself out of the thin air, but I had no idea how to stop.

CHAPTER 15

IT FELT FOR a long time that something bad was about to happen. Then one day, something did, something happened to Tony. We were accustomed to seeing Tony run in and out on his way to work, but one morning he did not go to work. He stayed in his cabin in Garden Court, muttering to himself in a loud voice, faster than normal talking, faster and faster. He moved quickly too. When he came out with his arms full of garbage bags, he looked like someone in a fast-forwarded video. He ran to the bins in the alley fast then back again fast. Then he put his radio on a rap station and turned it up loud so that Shae's windows rattled.

All of the residents of Garden Court came out to see what was going on except Grover, who was deaf. Grover could not even get out of bed by himself and the cabin doors were too narrow for a wheelchair. When the medical people came to take him in for a check-up, they would use two strong nurses and a metal walker to get him out of bed and set him up on the footpath. Even in the courtyard, his face seemed lit by a cool light, like moonlight. Grover might not have cared about Tony's music even if he could hear it.

Shae, on the other hand, came barreling out of her cabin, gave Tony a lecture, then called management to complain. The cooking lady and her new boyfriend called to complain too. Shae sat outside at the table to see if management would come promptly, but they did not show up. Eventually She went grumbling away on her day's expeditions.

Michael was not annoyed by Tony's behavior, he was alarmed. He carried his sandwich out to where Larry and I were sitting but when Tony rushed down the path with yet more garbage, Michael's eyes retracted into his head and he went into his cabin, clacked the lock tight, and did not come out all afternoon.

After Tony's third trip to the garbage, I walked over there to see what he could possibly be throwing away. The garbage bin was filled almost to the brim with everyday household goods in usable condition – books, dishes, clothes – plus some pretty nice items like a Sony Walkman and tapes and a little television about eight inches square. The bin looked like Santa's sleigh.

I stared at it, biting my lip until I tasted blood. None of the many things Tony collected had served him in the end, none had stopped his pain. I felt a strange kinship with him. I had abandoned my life too, thrown it out, all of it, when I came to the River, unable to pretend any longer that I was normal.

I turned to walk back and almost got run over by Tony

carrying out another batch. He did not react to seeing me there, just sped by, his face pale, his eyes dark and glittering; he dumped the armload and rushed back to his cabin.

Larry ventured over to look too and came back shaking his head. The next time Tony passed, Larry caught him and asked if he could take the little television. The boy looked at us for half a second, then said, "All garbage," and raced back to his house. Larry took this as an indication that Tony had no interest in the stuff. He rescued the little TV from the garbage bin and carried it tenderly into his cabin.

In time, Tony stopped carrying sacks out. I figured that he must have emptied all of the movable goods from his place. He closed up the cabin and turned down the music, but all afternoon you felt the tight, pushing energy in Garden Court, like energy in a room where people have been fighting. I wanted to take the dog for exercise, but it felt risky to leave Garden Court like that, so I agreed to play checkers with Larry and we played game after game.

Late afternoon, Tony walked out of his cabin and over to the picnic table.

"No work today?" Larry asked him mildly.

"Lies, lies, they think lies about me. Forget it," he said bitterly. "I don't need lies."

Larry asked him again about the TV, but Tony dismissed it with a wave of his hand. He started talking then, fast, about something his boss had said, what everyone else said, how he responded, but it did not hang together very well, and the words came out unevenly, fast then slow, hard to understand. Brutus, sitting at my feet, put his ears back in a fighting position.

As Tony was talking to us, the cooking lady walked under the trellis with a sack of garbage. Tony stopped his story and stood with his mouth hanging open, staring at her.

"They're coming. God!" he cried. He pulled a knife from his pocket, flipped it open and held it out in front of him. "No," he insisted as she approached. "I'm not going with you, I'm not! I'd rather die."

The cooking woman ignored this. She said good morning to us, then went on by to dump her garbage.

"They'll be back," Tony confided in a whisper. He did not put the knife away, but he let it drop to his side. "Those guys in white suits. They're looking for me. They'll be back."

I told him it was only his neighbor from the front cabin wearing a white apron. She had two children. She cooked for them and brought hot meals over to old Grover for a set fee the government paid her.

Tony listened and I thought the words were getting through, but when she reappeared from the garbage area, Tony fled screaming down the footpath.

"Higher than a kite," said the cooking woman briskly, returning to her own cabin.

I decided to phone management. I told them that the young boy living next to me was acting strange and that they should call his family or girlfriend or someone. The receptionist said that they had received four complaints about the music and that he would be out of Garden Court if it happened again. I asked to talk to Marcuzi. When he came on, he repeated what the receptionist had said but I explained that I was not calling to complain about that. I said this was something else. The boy had mistaken one of the residents for a man in white coming to take him away. He had pulled out a knife. The manager's voice changed. He said he would take care of it.

After I had notified management, I got my tire iron and took the dog out for a walk, a long loop that finished up at the abandoned park. Old Michael slumped on the bench under the apple tree, a bottle in his hand. He was upright but pretty drunk. While we were sitting there, one of the young Mexican men passed through the park headed toward the forest. When he saw my tire iron, he lifted a long knife out of a sheath he had on his belt and turned it over and over in his hand. Then he disappeared into the redwoods.

"Where's he going?" I asked.

"Hell," Old Michael said. "Like the rest of us."

I had the sudden feeling that I should get back to the cabin fast, and I ran all the way to Fourth Street. But by the time I got back to Garden Court, it was too late. I saw a police car and several men in uniform. As I passed under the entryway trellis, I heard the loud voice policemen use, and Brutus and I came running down the footpath just as they were dragging Michael from his cabin. His face was different, pale and plastic, and they carried him along like the nurses take Grover out, one big man holding him up on each side.

I started yelling from halfway up the footpath and by the time I got there everyone was staring at me. The policeman was the thin one with the mustache from the dogcatcher incident and he was rolling his eyes, but I rushed over to Marcuzi.

"You said the young man in the cabin next to yours," he said angrily, but he finally got the story straight and he signaled for the men to let Michael go and hurried over to him and brushed his clothes off. The men in white stepped back from Michael and they brushed him off a little too and he just stood there as if he were carved of wood and the policemen backed off and drove away.

That very evening, management sent someone over to apologize to Michael again and to offer him a month's free rent for the inconvenience, but it was never the same. I knocked on his door, but he would not open it. I spoke to him through the door, but he would not answer. He did not come out for lunch and he did not come out for dinner. It was a week later I saw him, late one night. He was muffled in clothing from head to toe, walking like a zombie out to the liquor store. A few days after that, his mother came to buy his groceries and she took him with her, and he did not come back.

CHAPTER 16

IT WAS HARD to get used to losing Michael. His absence was a black hole in Garden Court, and all joy got sucked into it and disappeared. But, for me, missing him was easier than the guilt. His cabin stood empty and accusing, and every time I went out to the picnic table, I remembered his warning to Butterball: "Better practice up, pup. Who knows what she'll do next?"

I replayed my phone call to management over and over in my head, making it clearer every time that it was not Michael, that Michael had nothing to do with it, but although the memory of the actual conversation slipped away, the towering guilt remained. Shae was more philosophical about it, saying Michael worried about being hauled away so much that it was bound to happen sooner or later. You cannot think about something so much, she said, without consequences.

What Shae thought about was her disability hearing: how they would attack her story and how she would stand by her truth in the face of all denial. When the day arrived,

Shae came out early to the picnic table, dressed in a new blue pants suit and prepared for every possible question. She appeared more excited than nervous, chain smoking and pacing up and down the deck, and her eyes flashed with indignation when she practiced responding to arguments opposing her own. As she was going over one more time exactly how she would respond if they accused her of making up her injuries, a stranger walked into Garden Court. He was a big, soft man, with heavy hips and thighs like you usually see on women. His hair was gray and curly like fine wire, and he had a bulbous nose, a little double chin. He dressed like someone from somewhere else, in a pale blue cardigan sweater with only one button fastened and brown leather slip-on shoes.

Shae stopped talking and we both watched his approach, but the man did not acknowledge our presence. He passed the veteran's cabin, climbed the deck stairs near Grover's cabin and directed himself to Vama's door like someone who had studied a map.

"Could be her son," Shae whispered. "He's supposed to live back east; pays the rent but too busy to keep in touch. Not even a call at Christmas."

The door opened and there was Vama. She looked like a small, wizened doll in her long dress belted with an apron. Her hair was braided as usual and each braid wrapped and pinned around her head like a crown, but still, braid and all, she did not come to the man's shoulder. She stood there silently looking at the man, her eyes narrowed and her mouth a thin line.

After a few minutes, Vama spoke, one or two sentences

perhaps, in a Slavic language. The man reached one arm awkwardly around her shoulders as if to hug her, but she stood unyielding. She said something else in that language, lifting her chin sharply in a gesture of demand. The man shrugged and put up his hands as one might at an unreasonable request or to indicate impossibility. At the same time, he glanced around Garden Court to see whether anyone was watching. When he saw us over at the picnic table, he moved slowly toward Vama, moving her into the cabin. The door closed with a brisk snap, but we could hear them speaking, mostly the man, for some time. He spoke partly in that Slavic language, and even Shae could not make out what was going on.

The man left about an hour later. By that time, Larry had wandered out, but the man did not glance over at the three of us, we just saw the back of the blue sweater, the swelling hips, and he was gone. Vama came out then. "Not son. No more son," she announced to us, shaking her head. Then she opened all the windows of her house, as if to air out the place.

Shae practiced her arguments a few more times then put on her good shoes and found her car keys. She packed up her papers into a stiff, new briefcase. We wished her luck and off she went. Larry strolled out to his van, walked back to his cabin and then closed the door. I went to work pulling weeds in front of the deck cabins.

Sometime later, Vama opened her cabin door and peered out. When she saw me, alone at the table, she shuffled across the deck closer to me. "No son," she said in a low voice to me, scowling. "I not now got son." Then she raised her hand and made a beckoning gesture underhand, like she was scratching the air. I walked up onto the deck, but she was making her slow way toward the cabin door. She paused, turned to me and beckoned again. I followed her in.

Vama's cabin was one room like Shae's, with the kitchen built into the far wall, but it looked very different. On one side, there was a round table with two chairs, a small sofa with crocheted doilies on the arms, and a television. On the other was a bed with a wooden frame. It was made up with a pillow and a navy blanket tucked in all round, and the white sheets were turned down over the blanket like an old-fashioned schoolboy's collar. A night table nudged up against it and I saw an old leather bible on top. On the wall behind it hung a boxy crucifix of pale wood.

Vama stood beside the bed. She waved me over impatiently with one hand; with the other, she lifted up the old, leather-bound bible. I reached to take it, but she did not hand it to me. She placed it carefully on the bed where it split open to reveal a photo inside. Like my own photo, it was in black and white, and the similarity gave me goosebumps. Her thin, wrinkled fingers trembled slightly as she handed it to me and mine were trembling too as I held it up to the light. The photo showed two rows of people, all with very solemn faces. Four children of differing ages sat on the grass in the front row, and three more children and two adults stood, unsmiling, in the back.

"Family," she told me, raising her chin and pursing her lips. She nodded twice, took the photo back from me, smoothed it with gentle fingers, then saw something else to show. "Homes to family," she said. I had to look carefully to see what she was pointing at: a one-story structure in the background with a sort of porch and a cow beside it.

Vama put the photo back in the bible and closed it up. She then crossed herself and reached up to take the crucifix down from its peg on the wall. It turned out to be a box. She held it with one hand and grasped Jesus with the other, sliding up the figure and, with it, the entire front of the cross to reveal a hollow space behind. In the lower part of the space was a glass vial of clear liquid, surely holy water. The top compartment was the same size and obviously destined to hold a similar vial, but instead there was a bit of cloth. Vama extracted the fabric and, glancing both ways over her shoulder, she held out the prize inside: a skeleton key. "Homes to family," she said, nodding. "Vama get in, yah. Family fine feeling shall see Vama."

The rest of the afternoon was filled with problems. Larry said his cat had disappeared and asked if I had seen it. I had not, but I took Brutus and looked for it down to the abandoned park. Larry stirred himself to walk out to search as well, but neither of us saw her, so I went over to the Vet Clinic to ask Jeff to keep an eye out.

Jeff was cleaning out the desk when I pushed the door open, and he rose to his feet, smiling. The desktop was piled with stacks of papers and odd items like pens, spools of thread, a package of instant coffee, a flashlight, little hotel soaps, beer bottle openers. The drawers of the desk sat on the floor, completely empty.

"It's the 'it-might-come-in-handy-one-day' syndrome,"

he joked, patting Brutus. "Dad insists that things be organized but he doesn't believe in throwing anything away."

I told him about Larry's cat disappearing and he jotted down her description. Just when he was done, the phone rang. It was obviously a client and I tried not to listen. Instead, I looked over the junk piled on the table. The flashlight was lime-green, just like my old one. I reached over and picked it up. It looked exactly like my old flashlight, but I could not be sure. I was still holding it when Jeff got off the phone.

"Another dog missing. Nothing but bad news today," he said grimly, then noticed I was holding the flashlight. "Need a flashlight? God knows where Dad found that thing. Please, do me a favor." I stuffed it in my bag.

When I got back to Garden Court, Shae was sitting out on the deck and flipping through a legal document, reading parts of it aloud to Larry. It was the new disability decision. Her hearing officer ruled that the pains in her neck were not related to her work, that they were all for convenience. Of course, how could he find otherwise when her own doctor testified that she was making up the story to compensate for other losses in her life. She ranted and raged for a time but after Larry went back into the cabin for Columbo, she sat silent and slumped. I could almost hear her plans and dreams crumbling and falling one by one as she turned them over in her mind: no physical therapy to make her body supple, no paralegal training, no little cabin of her own with tomato plants growing in the hot sun. I asked about possible appeals, but she did not talk much, and, after a while, she put on a coat and headed to the early AA meeting.

By the time she left, the temperature had dropped and a wind had come up. I went into my cabin. When Shae got back, she knocked at the window.

"Vama's taken off again," she told me. "I saw her over by Safeway with that suitcase on my way to the meeting. I'll go call management."

I was still cold, so I lay down on my mattress, bundled up in my sleeping bag with Brutus at my feet. I drifted off and dreamed that I was on a wagon train that was attacked by outlaws. When we heard the first shots, we pulled the covered wagons in a tight circle for protection, but we could not hold them off. They killed everybody except me and my young child. I tried to shield her, but the men caught me up, laughing. They bound my hands and the leader pulled me onto the horse in front of him and they rode off onto the desert. My child tried to follow on her small legs, her arms stretched toward me. But as the horses galloped out and away, she grew smaller and smaller, then she disappeared altogether in the distance.

The voice of a man woke me up and I hurled off the sleeping bag. It was still afternoon and the voice was Marcuzi from management, rapping on Vama's door and calling her name.

I stepped outside but Shae was out even faster. "She's taken off," Shae told the man sharply. "I already called to let management know. Doesn't anyone pass on messages over there?"

The man scowled at Shae and said he knew she had

called. He had taken the call himself. "But we can't find her," he snapped. "Maybe you would be so kind as to tell me where she's gone."

"Yugoslavia," Larry chimed in. The management man rolled his eyes.

"It's only been an hour or so," Shae said, looking at her watch. "She can't have got far, not with that suitcase."

"Well, maybe you'd like to go pick her up yourself," the man replied. "We poor fools were unable to spot her," he said. He tried Vama's doorknob, found it locked. "Do any of you folks have the key to her cabin?" he asked loudly. "We've misplaced the extra one at management."

I looked around to see who he was talking to and there was a crowd of Garden Court residents–Shae and Larry and myself, then the veteran and his mother. Even Grover's visiting nurse stuck his head out of Grover's cabin to see what was going on. On the other side stood the cooking lady with her new boyfriend; he had a scar down his cheek. His face looked familiar, but I could not place him.

"Do any of you have a key to Vama's place?" Marcuzi repeated slowly, as if he were speaking to a group of retarded people.

"She has a credit card," Larry said helpfully, pointing at me. Everybody looked over.

The man closed his eyes and shook his head as if asking the Lord for patience.

"Well, her son should be here soon," he muttered to himself. "Fortunately, he was held over looking at nursing facilities and did not leave this morning, as planned."

"That man from yesterday?" Shae asked.

"Yes, her son," the management man repeated, trying the door one more time. It was still locked.

"That's not her son," said the veteran. "Vama said it wasn't her son." The man rolled his eyes, shook his head, and walked out of Garden Court.

CHAPTER 17

EVERYONE HUNG AROUND Garden Court waiting to see what might happen except for Shae. She climbed into her old station wagon and disappeared. While she was gone, Garden Court filled up with men: policemen, firemen, the pudgy man who had visited Vama the day before, and two men from management. The vet's father walked in from Fourth Street. It looked like he had been called in from a job, since he wore work boots and old wool sweater. Marcuzi from management hurried over to fill him in. The other men went over too; they all seemed to know each other, and stood around in a circle, talking and joking. The policemen seemed reluctant to crack in the door, perhaps because of the fiasco with Michael, but finally their sergeant arrived with a signed authorization and they got ready. Two men held a metal pry-bar and they began to discuss where to insert it.

I saw Shae return through the trellis gate. She slipped over and said in my ear that she had driven up River Road herself, all the way to River's End, but no Vama. Just then the lock popped and the door opened in. The little room seemed so orderly and quiet, nobody wanted to go in. A policeman looked in quickly as if he thought Vama might be sitting there watching TV or something. Finally, the police sergeant and Marcuzi stepped inside to look around.

"Check the bathroom," the veteran called.

The men came out shaking their heads. Nobody.

"Let's get a search on," the sergeant said to a policeman. He got on his radio and began to talk. The sergeant ordered a canine unit to the cabin and a mounted search patrol as well as helicopter backup, and management organized volunteers. I saw the vet's father walk out with the pudgy policeman. Just beyond the trellis he paused, leaning over slightly. He blocked one nostril with the back of a big hand and exhaled sharply through the other, expelling mucus onto the footpath. I had seen someone do that before, and I wondered suddenly if it hadn't been my own father. How could I not remember?

Shae and I joined a search group with the veteran, the cooking lady and her boyfriend. I had Brutus with me on a lead. As we stood around waiting for instructions, the policeman with bloodhounds arrived, big dogs quivering with energy. The dogs sniffed the neat pair of sturdy shoes set out for them, began baying aggressively and took off up River Road.

Our group was to follow the dogs, then take alternative trails into the beaches or woods. We started out briskly and headed past Safeway, where Shae had seen Vama that morning. A light rain fell for a time, then hung in the cold air like a veil.

"That rain won't help the dogs," the veteran said.

We trailed the police team until the dogs left the road and descended into the woods beside the river. The baleful howls of the dogs grew distant as the dogs and their handlers travelled downstream, probably looking for a shallower spot to cross. Our group paused beside the road.

"She didn't go in the river," the veteran said. "Too cold, too old. She'll be looking for an easier way."

His voice carried well, and what he said made sense, but I was the only one listening. Shae had plunged into conversation with the scar face man. He was also in the Program, and they were comparing notes about another AA member someone had spotted buying a bottle at Safeway. Whenever the man turned, I eyed his face, trying to place it; the scar on his cheek went straight up in a line as if someone had cut him with a new blade. I knew that I had seen it before, that scar, that face, and it seemed sinister that the context had slipped away. Shae offered cigarettes to the man and the cooking lady and they started in on another AA drop-out, meandering down toward the river. The veteran tried to get them moving in the other direction a few times. Finally, he tapped my shoulder and gestured with his head. I followed him across River, then up a small trail on the other side that led back into the redwoods.

As we entered the forest, the woods closed behind us like a velvet curtain, silently, smoothly, and all that had existed back there was no more, and we moved farther into the deep of the forest. The veteran walked in front, light on his feet for his bulk, looking from side to side and down at the same time. His boots were army issue, black, with laces, and he carried an army backpack. I had never seen him look so vital. He seemed to absorb every element of the forest, the rich reddish-brown bark, the loamy smell, he drank it in with an intense concentration. Once he squatted down to peer at broken ferns, muttering to himself. Brutus seemed to be listening to him, his ears cocked toward him, his whole body quivering with the effort; I listened too but I could not make out a word.

The trail led us back into the woods, a clear trail, colored rust with redwood duff, smooth to walk on. Vama could have easily taken this trail and once I thought I glimpsed the gray blue of her coat up the trail, but it was only a tuft of huckleberries. The woods seemed quiet at first, then I began to hear noises: birds fluttering, a squirrel scampering through branches somewhere above, even a stream, although I could not see it, I could hear its rush and tumble through dark, close banks, its wild dash to the sea.

I stilled my mind and tried to sense Vama. I could imagine her standing in her cabin, her dish cloth over her shoulder. And I could place her in front of her family home in the photo. But here in the moist shade of the forest, I did not feel her. The veteran seemed to. He bent into his task and when he glanced back, his eyes glittered. His pace quickened to almost a run and I struggled to keep up. Brutus felt the surging energy, or something else, and he started growling low, a warning.

The veteran heard the growl and stopped. The dog was raising his muzzle to sniff, and the veteran, without speaking, peered intently in that direction, beyond the trail to the right where a rough path ran uphill between two redwoods.

He climbed the bank there and pushed between the trees. I followed, slipping on the duff. The path skirted a huckleberry thicket, then seemed to disappear, but the veteran found a way through and I stayed close behind, holding tight to the dog's leash. I could still hear the growling, but so very low I was not certain whether it came from the dog or the forest itself.

Some distance along, the path was blocked by a wall of trees. A large tree had fallen there and blocked our path. Other trees shouldered in tight and close, forming a complete barrier. The veteran squatted down to peer through the opening between the fallen tree and the ground. He said nothing but he must have seen something, because he stood up and worked to get on the other side. He fought his way around to the left, footsteps cracking in the dead branches, then scaled a second fallen log. Brutus and I were close on his heels. Finally, squeezing past a twisted madrone, we circled back into a clearing. I could see a slice of the sky again, heavy with low, dark clouds.

The veteran got his bearings, still without saying a single word. It was eerie and swallowed me up like a dream. Only the forest was real, only the veteran, alert, peering into the dusky undergrowth, pointing silently. We walked nearer. I finally saw it, a cat, a dead cat. Its body looked like it had been run through a meat grinder, but you could still see that its front paws were tied together with twine. We walked closer. Beside it lay the body of another cat, also mangled. This one I knew; it was Larry's cat, but it was missing more than an eye and an ear. Its head lay four feet from its body.

"Bait," the veteran said in a very low voice. "Blood training." The ground was deep stained with dark red. It was hard to believe the two little cats had that much blood in them. The horror of it started rising in me, but I put a quick lid on it and turned away.

We struggled back to the main trail and tramped on through the woods. The light of day filtered through giant redwoods created a twilight; or maybe it was twilight. It felt as if we had been searching there forever, all our lives and beyond. The trail went on and we went on, the veteran leaning over and fantastically alert, every sense open to the forest around him as if his life depended upon it, and my own urgency increased, the need to move through time, to be done with this, to confront whatever there was at the end, to see at long last the face of my enemy. The veteran did not talk at all now, not to me, not to himself, just proceeded at a run, hunched over, scouting the path. Path led to path and I felt we were far from River Road, far from Vama and Garden Court and the other searchers, somewhere in the landscape of a dream. Then, suddenly, the trail opened up into the familiar clearing of the abandoned park. We had circled deep around and approached it from the side. From above us came the sound of a police squad helicopter that was landing in the empty lot across the street, its search beam bright in the twilight and, behind, the sounds of men and dogs.

The veteran took in the helicopter, the dogs, all of it in just an instant, shielding his face with one arm. Then he leaped at me, tackling me, bringing us both down into a hollow of redwood needles behind a fallen tree. It was so sudden, so unexpected, that fear did not have time to strike, one minute I was squinting, blinking at the familiar abandoned park, the next I was sprawled on the ground beside a fallen tree trunk. Everything sped up then. Brutus started barking and I grabbed him and held him to me while the veteran shrugged out of his pack. He had his revolver out and ready, and he raised himself up to peer over the log, scanning the clearing. He held the gun with both hands, pointing it over the log.

"Keep down," he whispered.

I tried to stop him. In that moment, I saw clearly that he was not crazy, that his reaction made perfect sense given the screen of pain through which he viewed the world. I tried to get past the screen, talking low and precisely, telling him that he was not in danger, that his enemies were not upon him. I said that it was now, or, rather, that what he was feeling was not now. But for him it was, and just then one of the policemen ran in our direction and the veteran's gun went off and the cop hit the ground.

With the boom of the gun, I flattened myself on the ground, too, covering Brutus with my arm and shoulder. Another explosion, then other men running, and the veteran was out of there. Crouching low and signaling urgently for me to follow, he headed back into the woods. I could not have moved if I had wanted to. I lay on the ground with my dog, unable to move a muscle. Policemen charged toward the log with guns drawn. The next face I saw was the thin, mustached policemen who had chased racoons from under my cabin. He recognized me and rolled his eyes. "It's her again!" he said to someone behind him. "The one with the boogeyman."

It was hours later before I got back to Garden Court. The police finally got organized and took my statement and dropped Brutus and me off on Fourth Street. I went over to Shae's and found her watching TV with Larry. I told them about the veteran, what had happened, how last I saw he was running for the woods. But Shae had more news than I did, from his mother.

"They caught up with him, took him down," she said. "He's at Memorial, not in critical condition, only his leg got hit. But they're sure to keep him in the psych ward for a while at least, after shooting at the cops. Just lucky he didn't kill any of them. He'd be looking at a life behind bars."

"And Vama?" I asked. Shae shrugged and shook her head. She said they had searched until full darkness, a hard rain falling.

"No trace," she reported. "Nothing. Marcuzi said her son was to move her to a home at the end of the week."

"That's not her son," said Larry. "She said so."

"You can't believe everything said by a woman who thinks she can hike down River Road to Yugoslavia," Shae cracked.

"Well," said Larry, "it looks like she made it."

As I headed back to my own cabin, I saw that Vama's door was slightly open, red plastic ribbon barring it off as a crime scene. I walked across the deck, pushed open the door. Leaving Brutus outside, I stepped over the police ribbon into the cabin. It was too dark to see anything. I remembered the flashlight in my purse and brought it out.

The battery was low, but it provided enough light to see. The place had been ruffled, not torn apart. The crucifix was still on the wall over Vama's bed. I tiptoed over, took it down. As I slid up the lid, my hands trembled and the vial of holy water fell out and cracked open on the floor, forming a little pool. I looked quickly at the top chamber; it was empty. Vama had taken the key to the family home with her.

"Good luck Vama,' I whispered, but I did not really know what to hope for. Not that she would get back to Yugoslavia, because I knew her dream of home was a myth, a fairy tale concocted to mask the pain. Nor did I want her to be dragged back to a nursing home somewhere. In the end, I tossed the crucifix on the bed and returned to my cabin.

The police continued the search all night, but the morning brought no news and by the next weekend, all search efforts were halted. No trace was found of Vama, nor her suitcase, nor her keys.

CHAPTER 18

THE NEXT WEEK, I was called up to the police station to sign the statement about what happened with the veteran. On the way back, as I walked by the abandoned park, I saw a cat running toward the old apple tree pursued by two dogs. The cat was small, black with a white spot at the neck, and she ran fast. As she leaped at the trunk and ran up through the branches, red-brown curls of leaves flew from the tree, riding the air currents, first one direction, then the next, down to the ground.

The dogs arrived at the tree seconds later. They were pits or pit mixes, with huge heads, ears clipped close to the skull. They made no sound at all, just lunged up toward the cat. I felt a wave of heat, then cold and my fingers trembled, but the cat climbed well above the dogs' reach. I walked on, trying to catch my breath. The dogs would sit there for a few minutes, I figured, eventually go off and find something else to do.

Then I saw the dog's owner walking over to the tree. He was tall, heavy in a paunchy way, a muscular man gone to fat, wearing a white T-shirt. He did not look in my direction; his eyes were on his dogs and he bent into the walk, pushing off against a tall stick in his right hand. He marched so fast and angry, I thought he would hit the dogs with that stick, but he did not. The idea that he might see me was scary, as if just a glance in my direction would be the end. It was silly, but still I hurried over to the hedgerow at Fourth, then looked back to be sure he was not following.

He still stood under the tree with his dogs, so I took deep breaths, trying to calm myself. He stood there, the man, his walking stick raised up in the tree. My mind went blank for an instant, when suddenly the stick found its mark and the little cat came tumbling out of the tree. I could not move my eyes; I stared, saw distinctly how she recovered her balance, landing on her feet and running for brush all in one movement, hope against hope she ran. I felt the ice fear in her overwhelmed by the instinct to run, but the dogs were on her then, both dogs were on her, the dogs were on her before I could think anything, or do anything, or even know anything except that she was in two pieces; then I could move, and I ran back to my cabin. I lay on my mattress, body heaving with silent screams, insides aching, saw the cold bare room of my life below me, and was gone. When I came back, Brutus lay beside me, his muzzle on my heart.

That evening I told Shae. She said to call the cops, but I could not, they already considered me a nutcase. She then thought of the Society for the Prevention of Cruelty to Animals, but that was the pound, not a possibility either.

Then she called the cops herself, with me there listening, and they took a description of the man and the dogs.

"White guy, jeans, beer belly?" the lady cop on the phone repeated. "That could be any of a hundred men on the river. Seems these monsters should look different, doesn't it? Seems they should have a wolf head or fangs or something. That's why we never get them–they look just like everybody else."

It felt like the pace stepped up after that, as if bad things flew in packs like the dried leaves pushed from scrub oaks in the winter wind. The next day George walked in to see Shae and Larry, with a tight set to his face.

"No reason I could see," he said. "Morning all's fine, we're out hiking, laughing. Afternoon she buys a bottle at Safeway and is passed out when I come in for dinner." Larry looked disbelieving.

"Robbie?" he asked, as if he may have got it all wrong.

"Yes of course Robbie," Shae told him. "Who do you think he's talking about, his cat?"

"My cat's gone," Larry said.

"Robbie's gone too, old pal," George said. "'Get sober or get out,' I told her, and she made her choice real quick. Oh sweet Jesus, it can't be real."

"Have you called her sponsor?" Shae asked.

George nodded grimly. "He came over right away, was there when she came to. But she didn't want to talk, not to him, not to me. She went to take a shower, then out the back door."

After a time, Shae and George headed off to their meeting and I sat with Larry. He wanted to talk, but not about

Robbie. He seemed warmed up, open and relaxed, sitting there on his chair on the patio. Something taut inside him that I'd never really seen before had loosened and, in loosening, had drawn attention to its presence. Now as he sat, his legs fell slightly open, his shoulders relaxed back and down, and a subtle tightness in his face slipped and fell away. He began to talk suddenly, in a conversational tone, casually, as if he had always been a storyteller.

"My dad died in winter," he said. "He always said he would, then he did." Larry did not tell this sadly, more as an interesting fact. We thought about that fact and sat in the winter sun and watched the cooking lady's boyfriend carry out the garbage sacks to the bin. He nodded at us as he passed and Larry waved at him agreeably. This unfamiliar gesture so surprised the boyfriend that he stumbled and dropped a sack. As he bent down to retrieve it, I clearly saw his sliced face. I knew that face, but from where? I felt the need to know burn hot inside me. Suddenly, it came to me: In the newspaper, his was the photo that had been repeated over two opposite opinions of Clean Up week. That was it. It was nothing more than that. My own impuissance yawned before me like a bottomless chasm, all the twisting and turnings of my mind amounted to nothing, mere child's play.

"What happened to your face?" Larry asked the man convivially.

The man stared at this new, different Larry as if he expected him to sprout wings and fly away. "Hunting accident," he said, straightening up.

"What were you hunting?" Larry asked.

"I wasn't," he said. "These guys were."

"What were they hunting?" Larry asked.

"Me," said the boyfriend, raising his eyebrows. He picked up his garbage sack, nodded to us, and continued on his way.

"I used to go hunting rabbits," Larry told me cheerfully. "With my dad. But we never got one." He laughed, then refilled his glass from the Coke bottle. He did it so casually that Coke slopped over, onto the deck. Either Larry did not notice or else he did not care.

"I once went hunting deer with my high school principal," he said. "After my dad died." I thought this might lead him to sadder places, but instead he smiled big and warm.

"He was a real friend, my high school principal," Larry said. "A pal. They used to tell us to remember the difference between 'principle' and 'principal' because the princi*pal* was your pal. Well, he was." A woodpecker's tapping came from the top of the willow, tap-tap-tap in the clear, cold air. A spray of little blue birds flew down to the seed ball I had hung in a branch. One pecked at it; the others waited turns in the upper branches.

"When my dad died, I decided to quit school and sign up for the plumbers' apprentice program. So when the high school principal brings me into his office and asks me my plans, I tell him.

"'You should get yourself a high school diploma, son,'" he said. "He said 'son', just like I was his son. I told him the plumbers' program gave me a place to sleep and a job too. But he did not like that. He said that a high school diploma could help me out later in life. I tried to think about later in life, but I couldn't think past not having a place to stay after Saturday.

"'Son,' the principal says, 'they won't take you in that program without a high school diploma.' This was a real blow to me, and I didn't know how I'd make it. But the principal found me a room at the shop teacher's house and gave me a part-time job sweeping up after school, and every few weeks he'd take me out to do something, like hunting deer that day."

I listened to Larry and watched the little birds twitter and peck at the seed balls, some at the grains that fell to the ground. They were wary, the birds, glancing around before coming down to eat, one always keeping guard. The cat was gone and they were safe, but they did not know it.

"You know what?" Larry said. "When I went to sign up with the plumbers, I showed them my diploma, but the lady said you didn't need a diploma to join. The principal just smiled when I told him–he already knew it. He said that so I would get a high school diploma that could help me later in life."

He took out his wallet and extracted a folded paper. He opened it, carefully smoothed it out so I could see. It was his diploma, ragged at the edges, almost ripped through on the fold. We looked at it awhile, then he replaced it and sat there smiling, and we watched the cooking lady come out of her house carrying a tray for Grover. She tapped on his door, then went right in. A minute later, she walked out again, her face white and her eyes wide. "Lord rest his soul," she said. "Old man's gone."

There did not seem to be much to do so Larry and I sat

there and some women from management came over. After about half an hour an ambulance arrived. Two men went in, then one came out again to get a long, white-sheeted board, and they carried Grover's body out on it. The cot fit easily out the door. It was easier to get Grover out dead than alive. After a while, the police showed up and then management again and through it all Larry seemed to doze off in the rocking chair. More police came. It seemed like a lot of fuss since Grover was ninety-three, but the cooking lady told us that there was a strong smell of gas in the cabin and it looked like that's what knocked him off. It was strange, she thought, all the cabins were emptying out, one after the other.

"Always empties a bit in winter," the cooking lady said. "Now Grover. Well, there goes $50 a month," she said. "Sounds cold, I guess. Still, I liked Grover and he was no trouble and the money sure was nice to have."

I remembered the cool light that seemed to surround Grover's face and wondered where he was and where Vama was. Just then Brutus stood up and shook himself so that his little tag jingled and I knew it was time to take him out.

I left Larry with the cooking lady, snapped on the leash, and walked under the Garden Court trellis. On Fourth, I turned right toward management, passed Safeway, and headed down to the beach. I had a tennis ball and I threw it for Brutus a hundred times and each time he chased it. I arched it high so that the ball would bounce high into the air and Brutus would leap high into the air to retrieve it on the bounce. Sometimes I threw it into the river where it was shallow and slow, and Brutus paddled out to retrieve it, shake himself, then carry it proudly back to me.

I did not see Johnny approach. I heard a noise, turned, and he was walking down toward me from River Road. The fear slammed cold into me and almost knocked me over. Brutus heard the noise or sensed the fear and from way down the river beach he came running, speeding, to stand beside me. He did not growl nor bark, but his hair stood up along his neck and his muscles were tensed.

"Hey, calm down folks," Johnny said. "Just came over to say hello, friendly like. Tina's left, so a guy gets lonely."

I nodded slightly and, without turning my eyes from his, scanned the area behind, but there was no help in sight. Brutus did not move, nor change his stance.

"Hey," said Johnny again. "Want to get a coffee or something? My treat?"

I shook my head once. The man took a step closer and I backed away and the dog showed its teeth in a silent growl. Johnny raised his hands in the air as if in surrender.

"Okay, okay, forget the coffee. A guy sees when he's not wanted all right. But hey, when are you going to sell me that dog? I'm ready to pay a fair piece now. Weren't before, I admit it. But I've checked around and I'm willing to go to $300 now, not bad for a mix that's too small to ever be a real top dog."

I frowned and shook my head again.

"How about $400?" Johnny said. "Last offer." He read the answer in my eyes.

Johnny bent low toward me, as close as he dared with Brutus standing there. "You know I'll get what I want now or later little girl," he said in a sort of whisper, putting his hand around my forearm as if to hold me there. "I need that dog and I need it soon. I'm being a real gent about it, asking nice, willing to pay, but I'm not always so gen-teel. You ask Tina about it sometime, 'bout what I can do if you get me mad."

I tried to move, but I could not move. My legs did not respond at all, my arms were paralyzed. I felt a desperate need to flee but I could not, I was trapped there in the prison of my body, my heart thumping and the crazy distance coming over me. I felt myself slipping, slipping and suddenly I could see my body below and Johnny, then Shae.

Shae? Shae! Shae was up at River Road, yelling on down to me, waving her arms toward me. Johnny disappeared, and I was back in my body, heading up toward Shae, Brutus behind me.

"What are you up to?" Shae said. "Meeting just got out. You'll never believe what I heard about Robbie."

I was breathing as if I had run up a mountain, each inhale so ragged it felt like my lungs must be scratched and bleeding from the effort. Shae did not notice. She took a cigarette from her purse and set about trying to light it, and I forced my body to take slow, deep breaths. I looked back down toward the beach and it was empty. Nobody. Nothing. One more time I had escaped from nothing. It was as if I had created it all out of the clear, winter air.

Shae succeeded in sucking life into the cigarette. As we walked back toward town, she hurried to pass on the fresh news. "Robbie started drinking, you know that. But this you don't know. She took off with Jack!" I must have had a blank look on my face. "Jack," Shae repeated. "Our old handyman, remember? The one who was going places. Well he's gone somewhere, direction of Texas, with Robbie beside him in the Chevy. Now what do you make of that?"

"They said Robbie fell for his music, used the booze to make the break. She fell for Jack's music! Can't imagine it," Shae said, shaking her head. "*Cannot* imagine it unless his 'repertoire' improved a lot since Larry's birthday."

I remembered his birthday then, the cake. How long ago summer seemed, as if it had taken place in my childhood. We walked slowly in the cool afternoon air. I told her about Grover dying, the gas smell.

"They're dropping like flies around us," she said. "Old Grover gone; well that explains why the cooking lady didn't make the meeting. Everyone wondered. She never misses."

We stopped at the Post Office and Shae retrieved a couple of letters from her box. Then we headed over to Safeway where a little girl with ponytails was sitting on the sidewalk giving away kittens. Shae needed to buy stuff since she had asked George to dinner. I could not go into Safeway with the dog nor would I leave him alone outside, so I took a walk past the park. Michael and Mickey were there. I waved a greeting but did not go down; Michael would see right away that, once again, I had just barely escaped with my life.

CHAPTER 19

THE DAYS GREW shorter, but each stretched out barren as a desert. I stopped going to the cafe since I could not take Brutus inside. Instead, I would buy a coffee to go. The hot cup burned my hand as I walked with it, reminding me I was still alive. With my coffee and the dog and my tire iron, I went to the abandoned park. Sometimes I would see Michael, but often I came and went before he arrived.

One morning, a cold wind blew in from the west and the air sighed with rain. I arrived at the park about sunrise and apples lay strewn across the ground as if someone had shaken the tree like a wet umbrella. I scanned the field carefully, from the first line of redwoods to the road, scanned it like a soldier might scan the horizon for an enemy figure. Nobody. I let Brutus off the leash and he wriggled for joy in his freedom, shook from head to tail, then stood before me expectantly, wagging his tail. I selected an apple from the ground and threw it toward the forest. It went a very long way, arching over the field, then hitting and bouncing but Brutus was on it after the first bounce. The second time it went further.

"Strong arm," a voice said behind me and fear smacked white into me like the palm of a big hand, spinning me around–just old Michael, heading down from the alley with Mollybelle and his breakfast beer. Just old Michael, I said to myself, just old Michael, but the panic was harder to check; it had already taken hold, spreading like wildfire. Brutus dropped the apple near my feet and stood waiting, every muscle in his body ready. I picked up the apple and tossed it again, just to do something so Michael would not see. But he had already seen.

"Bad moon rising," he said. "Strong lass like you, what else you got to walk with than that fear?" He settled into his usual corner of the bench beneath the apple tree, setting his accordion case beside him, his beer on the flat rock he had organized long ago.

Brutus chased down the apple and I threw it again, a clear arc in the quiet space. Michael and I both watched it soar, watched the dog retrieve it, tumbling over in his furor to play. He brought it back, mashed beyond repair, so I choose another and let it fly. Michael chugged on his beer, then whistled appreciatively as the apple almost entered the dark wood beyond the park.

"Strong lass," he said again. "They couldn't kill it off, could they? Like a tree with the strength inside. You can hack up the bark, cut off limbs, but the real strength is inside, the sap, the push to grow." I said nothing, just threw that apple over and over, then another one, then another.

But now I could feel the muscles in my arm, in my back, as I threw.

"Yes, child, bad moon rising." Michael said after a long time. "Hunters' moon, blood moon. Old enemies at the door, bloodletting, shadows. My Mollybelle's afraid, won't leave my side."

Above the redwoods in the early morning sky was a thin moon, a curl of a moon, pale but sharply cut like the old scar of a deep wound. I shivered. Michael finished his beer then brought out his accordion from the bag. He played, the notes complex and sorrowful in the empty morning. The dogs gathered round and we listened to the music, floated up on that music. I felt tears rising in me and bit the inside of my cheek angrily.

Suddenly, Brutus turned toward the road, alert. A stumbling shape appeared on the path from the alley to the park. It was Mickey, but disheveled, rough, hulking, his pants torn at the knee and his red plaid shirt buttoned wrong so that one side of the front hung long and the other short. Michael put down his accordion and pulled out another beer.

"Bad moon, child," he muttered.

"Have ye seen me Lulabelle?" Mickey asked in his husky voice as he approached. His face was very white, like in cartoons. "Me old girl, where might she have got to?"

We had him sit and he told us about his night–he'd had enough for a bottle, so he bought one at Safeway and he downed it with pleasure out at Johnson's Beach with Bear, playing cards. Lulabelle was right by his side. He did not remember much after that, leaving the beach, saying goodbye to Bear, Bear crying like a baby so Mick going along with him to the benches behind Safeway and telling more stories, then Bear passing out and him heading back to his car with Lulabelle.

"Then what?" asked Michael.

"Then nothing," said Mickey, looking down at his hands, the fingers curled slightly, puffed like sausages. "Then I wake up, all warm, but not warm enough, something's missing and I sit up and bump my head hard and then I see that Lulabelle's nowhere down there. Usually she's there, looking up at me, saying 'Ga morning.'"

"Did you leave her somewhere last night?" Michael asked sternly. "I tell you, real drinking should be done near where you're going to sleep. Did you leave her with Bear?"

Mickey shook his head, then batted it with the palm of his hand as if to shake up some memory in there that was not in its proper place. "I can't say for certain, but I think she was following me toward the car."

Michael glowered and Mickey bent his head low, covering his face with his hands. I said we should go over to his car and look for clues, so we walked over to the parking lot behind the old bank, Mickey limping just behind us. I inspected the car Mickey lived in but there was nothing like a clue, just an old station wagon with blankets and a sleeping bag in the back, the front seats filled with empty bottles, clothes, some papers. They decided to go to see Bear behind Safeway, so I went along, but he was still passed out. On the ground beside him, something sparkled. It was a bell like the ones on Lulabelle's collar. Mickey picked it up and held it tight in his hand.

I wanted to do something yet there was not much to do. Mickey shook Bear harshly, but he did not stir. Finally, Michael went down to River Road to play his accordion and Mickey staggered over to the Church Center to clean up a bit and get an aspirin. I decided to tell Jeff that Lulabelle was missing.

"How's that handsome mutt?" Jeff asked as Brutus and I walked in together. He was drinking a coffee at his desk and going through mail, but he stopped and poured me a cup. Then he patted Brutus' head and rubbed behind his ears. When I told him about Lulabelle, his cheery tone passed and his voice became carefully neutral.

"Not likely to turn out well this story," he said. "I don't like to say it, but the most likely news will be bad news. I'm up to my eyeballs in dead and mutilated cats, missing dogs." He stopped and got himself more coffee, then beckoned me into the back room where a young beagle lay in a box on a blanket.

"She came in last night," he said calmly. "Clearest count possible, fifty-eight bites, lost an eye, both ears chewed off. Probably won't make it." I gagged and turned back to the reception area. The horror hit in succeeding swells, each one sufficient to knock me off my feet. I collapsed on the sofa.

Jeff followed me, sat down beside me. "They blame it on pits but it's not the pits," he said. "Left alone, dogs might rough it up every now and then, but they would never tear each other apart."

Something about his calm voice enraged me. But when I turned ferociously to him, I saw that his arms were folded tight across himself as if to keep his guts from spilling out, his face twisted up, his eyes smoldering.

"I know why they do it, those pits," he continued, in the same, level tone. "They do it to please the men that own them, out of their great love. Makes me think of the seminary," he said. "You know, they took me when I was ten years old. They have the nose for it."

I tried to say something, but he cut me off. "It happened, it happened," he said, turning his head away and pressing his arms against his body until the fingers turned white with the effort. "Anger is not a big part of my life," he said. "But it's hard to see what they do to these dogs and not feel something."

He stopped, shaking his head as if to reprimand himself. "Sorry," he said. "It's just hard, that's all. I hope Lulabelle's wandering the streets fat and fine, and maybe she is. I'll let you know if I hear anything. Bad or good." He bent down and scratched Brutus behind the ears. "You take close care of this fellow," he said. "He's already paid his dues."

I took Brutus home and locked him in the cabin, then headed to Safeway to pick up something to eat. Right in front of the store, ten feet from where the little girl sat with her kittens the week before, sat Bear. He was swigging a beer and arguing with Mickey. Mickey stood over him, swaying and talking loud. He did not appear to have made it down to clean up.

"Don't know, Mick," Bear was saying. "Don't know for sure but I never knew you to take off without Lulabelle. You're never leaving that dog nowhere, now are you man? Never seen you leave that dog nowhere."

As I was hurrying over, a police car streamed in, cutting me off. I walked right up, then saw it was the two cops who found the raccoons under my cabin, so I pretended to look at the rack of newspapers nearby.

"What's up boys?" said the cop with the mustache "Those ladies in Safeway don't like you two out here discussing matters."

"He took my dog," said Mickey, beginning to cry right there, in front of the cops, Bear and the lady from Safeway who peered out the door.

"Did not," said Bear. "I passed out before him so how could I have done it."

"Whoa now," said the fat policeman. "Lulabelle's gone? Where's she got to then?" But Mickey sobbed so hard he could not answer. I blocked off my shame at seeing the policemen and stepped over to explain. I told them how they had been playing cards, how Mickey woke up without the dog, how Lulabelle's bell was on the ground near Bear. I saw the mustached cop remembering me, saw it all in his eyes. I finished what I had to say, then fell silent.

"So, Mick's without a dog," said the fat cop.

"Do we suspect anyone this time?" the first one asked me.

"You don't really think I took your old girl," Bear said to Mickey. "You don't really think that, do you buddy? I'm a rotten drunk and I cheat at cards but steal a guy's dog?"

Mickey put his arms around Bear and sobbed, "No, Bear, course you're right. I'm just all lost without me girl."

"Well," I said, "someone took her, she didn't just

wander off leaving her bell behind. Someone took her and she's somewhere."

The cops looked grave. "There's been a lot of bad news coming into town lately," said one. "Pick-up dog fights, dead cats, even a pack of dead kittens." He lowered his voice as if to keep the news from the little girl who had offered her kittens the other week, even glancing to where she had been sitting. "We're thinking there's a big roll planned soon, since they're looking for blood animals, to excite their rollers, see." Mickey let out a sound that was half shriek, half groan.

"Now, Mick, that's not to say Lulabelle's ended up ground round. You go over to Charities and get cleaned up a bit, get something inside your belly beside sixty proof. We'll look around a bit see if we spot the old girl."

They sent Mickey on his way. I went into Safeway, but the smell of meat permeated the place and I felt sick. I bought a cheese sandwich then hurried back to Garden Court to make sure Brutus was okay. Before I unlocked the front door, I peered in the window. Brutus stood, teeth bared, quivering slightly. But when he saw me, he raised his muzzle and lifted a paw. I rushed to him and told him I would protect him, and he stopped trembling enough to eat my cheese sandwich.

I could not leave it alone, I wanted to, but I could not. After walking Brutus that evening, I locked him in the house, took my tire iron and headed down River Road past Safeway, then back into the woods on the trail the veteran and I took a few weeks before. It was dusk. My footsteps sounded loud in the quiet wood, no rain, no breath of wind. Fallen redwood needles lay in wet orange heaps on the path. I kept walking, slowly but steadily, the tire iron marking time against my leg, until I reached the side trail that led to the clearing where we had seen the cats. I pushed up the bank, crept in toward the fallen redwood, my steps light and stealthy. I was almost at the tree when I heard something. I stopped, stopping footsteps, stopping breath, stopping all sound. Someone was in the clearing.

Ice flowed through me with the adrenalin, followed by an urge to run. I blocked it, pushed it aside, ordered myself to calm. They have not seen you. Take a look first. See if Lulabelle is there. I took a deep breath. I smelled dogs, tobacco smoke. Bending down low like the veteran had, I could just see into one edge of the clearing through the low window between the redwood trunk and the ground. I saw two dogs, two pit bulls, struggling. The bigger one had chomped down on the muzzle of the younger dog and was whipping its head back and forth. The younger dog's eyes were wide. It tried to free itself, and blood flowed down its velvet nose, pooling on the ground. The pup was black as the shadow dog. It began to whine now, a sad, small sound.

"Isn't that enough for the pup?" said a voice. "He'll get himself killed sure." From my viewpoint, I could not see the speaker, only his legs from the knees down, long shorts, high-top tennis shoes. I did not dare to try for a better view.

"Your dog now," said another male voice, farther away. "But that's not how you blood it. If it can stand, it can fight." The man stopped and I heard the scrape of a match, then a strong smell of cigar smoke. I could not see that man at all, but I heard him continue.

"This pup should be game, out of that young bitch with bloodlines to Mayday from my Shadow of Death." I realized with a kind of thrill that he was probably talking about the shadow dog. "That bitch is a killer herself," the man went on. "Had to put her in the rape box to let Shadow do his job."

They stood and watched the dogs, and I watched too, all of us watching together, united by the violence we were witnessing. Bending down there, unseen, invisible, dead inside, I watched until the pup stopped struggling. It might have been ten minutes, might have been an hour. All I knew is that I was there when he collapsed, almost softly, to his knees. Only then did the top dog give up its grip, taking a better one on the young dog's neck, flipping him to his back, pinning him there, teeth in his throat, blood everywhere.

The man in shorts grabbed a long wooden pole from somewhere beside him, jammed it into the big dog's mouth, between its teeth. He pried the dog's jaws open, grabbed its collar, hauled it off. The young dog lay still. The other man stepped over and the bottom of his legs came into my range of vision, tan pant legs, white leather saddle shoes, lace-ups. The front and back were white, the middle black. As he gave the dog a shove with one foot, I saw cleats on the sole. His shoe pushed the pup's body, and I saw it stain red on contact, the red spreading slowly up the toe as the leather absorbed the blood. The young dog struggled to its feet, muzzle and neck slick with blood. He just stood there panting, looking straight ahead.

"What you think?" the owner asked.

"He's had enough," the older man told him. "He's in shock."

My hands trembled and my teeth tried to chatter. I felt myself slipping away, the distance soaring out around me. I had to get out of there, get out quickly. I had learned nothing, but I could not stay any longer. As I staggered to my feet, the forest revolved around me. Everything was off balance, and my heartbeat was deafening. I began backing away shakily, silent steps back toward the main trail. I was almost there when a bush knocked against the tire iron and it fell on a slab of rock with a clang.

"We got company," one of the men said loudly, and I heard a scrambling. I took off running, then, sprinting at top speed, past trees and more trees, coming at last to the side of the abandoned park. Nobody was there. I limped over to the apple tree, leaned against it panting, feeling its calm, its strength. The violence skittered inside of me, and I did not know how to stop it. Tell your sorrows to a tree, the Indians say, when you have no one to tell, tell your troubles to a tree and it will help you. But what was my trouble? The frightening men and their inhuman behavior? The dog fight? I suddenly realized that, at the core, it was not the men, nor was it the dogs, not even the shadow dog; it was something inside me, my own towering fear. I was running from dangerous men, but I could as easily be fleeing from bats, evading the cooking lady, exchanging gunfire with invisible enemy soldiers.

"I am afraid," I whispered to the tree. "Every moment, every day. I am afraid he will get me, and I do not know who and I do not know why." A white flash of emotion shook me, a whirlwind of white, then it was gone. I walked round to the bench then, sat there and watched evening sweep across the park, dark drapes drawn on the world, watched light fade and night come, watched bats flutter across the twilight, curving off sharply after insects. Here was an owl, calling from the wood. Some see better in the dark than in the light. It is a different way of seeing, a sensing of shades and shapes; an intuiting of what is, from shadows and deeper shadows. At night, details are not important.

I walked up to Fourth Street, up to Jeff's office. It was closed up tight. I remembered Brutus then, waiting for me, and headed back to Garden Court. As I walked under the trellis, I sensed a shape near the picnic table. It was Larry, sitting at the picnic table in shirtsleeves.

"Have you seen my girlfriend?" he asked me.

"Isn't Shae at her meeting?" I said.

"Not Shae. The little dark-haired girl I've been with since Shae left me," he said.

"Shae left you?"

"Couple years ago. So I'm with this little dark-haired girl, works as a waitress."

I realized that Shae had been right about the medication. They called her stories apocryphal, but they were true. I felt a jolt of triumph for her, for us all, the bitter triumph of a bitter truth. I looked at Larry and he looked at me, his eyes wide and dreamy. Then he got up and went into his cabin.

They found Lulabelle's body the following week,

punctured by a hundred bites. Her muzzle was almost chewed off. Jeff came by Garden Court to tell me.

"She couldn't have lasted very long," he said bitterly. "That's the only good part, she could not have lasted very long. Cops say its Mexicans, but I say it's all-American scum. Cops say a big fight's planned around here sometime soon; they say some terrible stuff will happen, but I say it's already happening, it's been happening for years."

I went to sleep that night and dreamed of my father. I could not see his face; it was in shadow. He was filling his pipe with tobacco, slowly, slowly, stuffing more and more into the cup of the small pipe until I thought it would burst. Then he set it afire.

CHAPTER 20

A FORTNIGHT OF RAIN and no end in sight. The river was high, not near flood levels but still, fear hung in the air with the rain. You could feel it more than see it, feel it cold on your skin as you walked down River Road, as you passed the coffee shop, as you shopped at Safeway. The ground was saturated, any rain would be enough.

Every day the bulletin board in front of Safeway held new notices about lost dogs. Dogs were missing up and down the river. The newspaper attributed it to the full moon eclipse coming up, which, they said, drove animals crazy. Even animals from the pound disappeared. The director of the pound agreed that dogs felt the moon's pull, but he said he doubted that it was the man in the moon who had used a blow torch on the cage doors. He said dog fighting was a reality whether you wanted to think about it or not, and that it was just as likely to be your father as some Mexican down the street.

I went up one afternoon to see Jeff, to tell him what I

had seen in the woods. Shame overwhelmed me. I had done nothing, I did not even have information to report: Two dogs I did not know, two men I did not see. Still I took Brutus up and Jeff was alone in the den, playing his guitar, and I sat on the one chair and told him the story.

"All you saw was the feet?" he asked. "High-top sneakers and white saddle shoes, right toe stained with blood?"

I nodded.

We sat there without talking, and he tuned up his e-string, then got up and poured us coffee. He'd picked up real mugs somewhere, and mine was warm against my palms. For some reason, I thought of my mother, rising from bed to make coffee when visitors came as if everything was okay.

"It always seems to help, doesn't it?" Jeff said and grinned, raising his eyebrows. "I can bear anything as long as I wash it down with coffee. So, you saw their shoes. Anything else? I thought about it, shook my head. "Anything about their voices distinctive? Any cars in the area?" Again, I shook my head. He sighed and we were silent for a time. "Well," he said finally, "at least you tried. And you never know, you might see those men again," he said. "Or rather, their shoes." The men's shoes seemed a dark image, but Jeff laughed so young and clear when he said it that I laughed with him as long as I could. Then I went back to Garden Court.

I did not go out much those days after Lulabelle, I stayed in the cabin with Brutus. Garden Court was a ghost town, so many empty cabins. Brutus was wary. He stayed by my side, a part of him touching a part of me night and day. It was hard to know where I stopped and he started. I never left him alone now. I stopped going to the cafe and stopped going to Safeway; it was too dangerous to leave him outside. Shae picked up what I needed at Safeway while Brutus and I stayed with Larry. Shae did not want to leave Larry alone either, although she kept telling herself she had to let go and let God.

I never saw Larry take the pills, nor did Shae and she watched him like a hawk. Still, he was high most of the time, hallucinating or sleeping. His eyes lost the wondering brightness and were soft, foggy. He was always looking for people who were not there: his dad, his high school principal, even his brother Harry which drove Shae nuts.

"Harry is a rapist, a sadist, a murderer," I heard her screaming one day. "He's in prison for sixteen years, Larry. Stop asking him to turn up the TV."

Of course, Brutus had to go out, and I went out with him, up River Road, past the cafe, looping around by the park and home. Sometimes I still took him to the park to chase apples and sometimes Michael was there and we spoke, but Mickey was never there anymore. He began hanging out with Bear and his group, drinking the hard stuff. It was as if the stature of being one of the tramps with dogs had kept him from falling over the edge and once it was taken from him, he fell. Maybe it was the weight of the sorrow. Someone from Charities brought him a new dog, young and cute, but he would not take it. At first, the cops gave him a break, but when he got caught a second time lifting a bottle at Safeway, they hauled him in. After a week he was back, but never really back.

Little Michael came back one weekend, but he was never really back either. His mother had kept the cabin for him when he was ready and then I guess he was because one rainy Saturday she brought him back with a couple of bags of groceries, and he locked himself in. We hardly saw him at all, yet sometimes I could feel him again, watching through the walls.

The winter rain turned the path leading up the center of Garden Court into a bog and nobody walked in if they did not have to. The cooking lady put on boots to bring her garbage back to the bins. I put on boots to take Brutus out.

One day after I finished walking Brutus, I stopped by Jeff's office to say hello. He was in the back room on the phone, so I sat down on the couch, looked at the fashion magazines. All those pretty girls, pretty smiling faces. Was there ever a time that I had been like everybody else? I could not remember one, but memory was not my strong suit. The front door opened and in walked Jeff's dad, carrying an umbrella in one hand, a pair of golf shoes in the other. He smiled at me warmly.

"You're a bright spot in this wet day," he said. Tossing the shoes and umbrella on the low table, he leaned over and shook my hand. Then he turned to hang his raincoat on a peg on the back of the door. As he took it off, I smelled male sweat and cigar smoke. I searched for something to say.

"No golf today?" I finally managed.

"Optimist though I am," he said, smiling, "I really wasn't counting on playing golf today. I'm just taking in my golf shoes to have them cleaned, since it looks like I won't be needing them this week."

He started flipping through mail at Jeff's desk. I tried to think of some graceful way to leave, but everything I came up with seemed contrived. I stared awkwardly at the door, then at the umbrella. The umbrella was dripping all over the magazines, water running across the pretty faces, so I picked it up and set it tip down on the carpet. Then I thought better of it, after all it was his clinic, not mine, so I leaned over silently to replace it beside the shoes. The umbrella was blue; the golf shoes were white and black. Suddenly, an electric thrill ran up my spine. I sat up tall, motionless, looking harder at the shoes, harder. It seemed as if nothing existed in the entire universe except the shoes. The toes were white, both a little dirty. But the right shoe had a stain on the toe, a stain the color of autumn leaves.

Slowly, like in a dream, I reached my hand out toward the shoe. Carefully, carefully, I moved my fingers around to the back of the shoe and lifted it off the table. There were cleats on the bottom of the shoe. Electricity whirred around the room now; my face was hot, my ears rang. I brought the shoe toward me. The toe of the right shoe was stained with blood.

I do not know how long I sat there, staring at the shoe. I heard Jeff's dad speaking to me, saying something about the shoes and how it was hard to keep anything clean. His voice went on and on, then it stopped. He came over and, almost gently, removed the shoe from my hand, returned it to the table.

I looked up at his face. I felt a floating sensation, nothing more. "You," I said. "The shadow dog belongs to you."

Jeff's dad stood there for a long moment, as if weighing

the alternatives, then he sat down on the couch beside me. "So, it was you, there in the bushes," he said, looking at me appraisingly. The voice was even, pleasant, but hard underneath. "You should be careful," he continued. "It can be dangerous for a little girl in the woods after dark. It's always a better idea to mind your own business. Didn't your mother teach you that?"

He shook his head in resignation at the way young people were being educated, then took a cigar from his pocket, trimmed it and lit it. After he had sucked it into life, he began speaking again, low. "Or maybe you're interested in working dogs yourself. You could make yourself some money with that dog; he has quite the reputation." He sat with his chin on his fist, his eyes locking mine.

I did not answer. I was thinking of the little pup, falling to his knees, I was thinking of Jeff. My eyes must have turned slightly toward Jeff's office, because the man raised one eyebrow at me, derisively. I felt my face flush with fear or something else.

"Go ahead," he said. "Jeff will never believe you. You know that already, don't you? Nobody will believe you."

"Nobody will believe what?" came a voice from behind me. Jeff had come out of his office. He stood behind the couch; his dad tipped his head up toward him and smiled. Then he hefted himself up and walked around to shake his hand.

"Hey Dad, great to see you," Jeff said. "What line are you feeding the clients today?"

"Your little friend has been playing dogfight detective,"

he said. "She's making some pretty serious accusations against your old dad."

He laughed, an amused male laugh, and Jeff laughed with him. I felt his eyes on my back, but I did not turn around or speak. Jeff stopped laughing.

"You're kidding," he said, whether to myself or to his dad, I could not say.

"Women," his dad said, shrugging.

Jeff walked slowly around the couch, his eyes searching my face. He stopped a few yards away. "You are kidding, aren't you?" he said.

I did not look up. I knew what was going to happen. I knew what was at the end of this road, but I could not pull away from it, there was no pulling away from it this time. Fear was palpable in the air, I could feel it mixing and mingling with Jeff's energy, with my own, turning everything thick, muddy, as if the room was crowded with ghosts. I leaned over slowly, picked up the shoe again, held it up so he could see. Jeff looked for a minute, really looked. I felt hope flicker in me, a faint hope like the flicker of a match in the black night. Then he glanced at his father; something closed in his face and the match went out.

Jeff took the shoe, held it to the light. "That's not blood," Jeff said, shaking his head. "Blood is thicker. That's . . . ." The silence seemed to last for a full minute. He looked over at his dad.

"Coffee," his father said, sitting back at the desk and starting to sort mail.

"Cof–fee," Jeff said, drawing out each syllable and nodding as if it were the answer to a riddle he had been struggling with for a long time. "It's only coffee," he told me, shrugging. I said nothing. Nobody said anything. Finally, Jeff spoke.

"Speaking of coffee," he said cheerfully, "I just put some on. Who wants a cup?"

I took Brutus and left, out of the Bordeaux Vet Clinic, out onto Fourth Street. Heavy rain fell for a time, then turned into mist. I walked aimlessly around the cafe, then past the park. Old Michael was there, and I went down with Brutus and sat on the wet ground, my back against the tree. Michael saw I had taken a hit, but he did not say much, just pulled out his accordion and began to play. I closed my eyes and tears streamed down my cheeks. Brutus pressed against me, and I heard the wind high in the redwoods, felt something cold and hard and treacherous twist in the very center of my heart.

CHAPTER 21

THE MORNING OF the full moon, something was different. I lay still on the mattress, listening. After a while, I realized that it was the brush of the rain, its low song, gone. All was still, no wind, no rain, no noise from Garden Court. It felt like someone had turned life off like a television set.

I stood up and looked outside. Night still occupied Garden Court. The winter sun would not rise for hours yet and I had a sudden urge to go to the cafe, drink a coffee and read the paper as before. I wanted things as they were before. But before what? Before Jeff? Before Michael? Before the flood? There was no beginning to this, it had been with me forever, I knew it, it had been with me as long as I could remember and before that. It had worn different faces, different cloud cover, but beneath it all, it was the same. There was no before, no after, just the darkness.

I got up in a fury, dressed and hurried out with the dog on a leash. I walked up to Armstrong Woods Road through the gray light, strode past the vet clinic, then headed over to the cafe. I marched into the cafe with Brutus, right past the No Dogs Allowed sign, daring anyone to say anything. The man gave me an odd look but said nothing, and I sat down and read my paper, feeling defiant, strong as the world. The two cops came in later, but they did not say anything about the dog either, they just spoke together about the moon.

"Brings out the crazies," one told the cafe man. "Always more trouble during a full moon, let alone an eclipse. I for one am taking the evening off." He put a heaping spoon of sugar in his coffee. "Old lady's sick, needs me," he said, winking at the man behind the counter.

I sat in the cafe and drank my coffee and read the paper. It felt like going home. The paper talked about the rain, the flooding, the eclipse. One article explained that a lunar eclipse occurs when the earth lines up directly between the sun and the moon, blocking the moon from direct sunlight. As the moon passes into the earth's shadow, its visible face gets smaller and smaller and finally disappears. Only red rays filter through the dark umbra, so the eclipsed moon turns red when it enters the darkest part of the shadow of the earth.

I tried to understand it. Where light is not, that's a shadow. You could see some things more clearly by looking at their shadows than looking at the things themselves. The things themselves might blend in with other things, be blown about, confused, but a shadow was clear and precise as a scar. I felt I finally understood it and I reached down openly and patted the dog under the table. Just then Shae marched into the cafe and called to me across the room:

"Hey, what's Brutus doing in here?" My defiance slipped away like rain down the window.

Shae stumped over to my table with her coffee like a gnome going to battle. She had an appointment with a new lawyer, a specialist in psychiatric malpractice. "After all, Larry's my husband now," she told me.

Neither she nor Larry had ever talked about a marriage. But now she admitted she'd done it two weeks ago, dragging Larry along to City Hall. "It's for him," she said, a little defensively. "Now, maybe, I'll have some say in his treatment, or, anyway, if not, his shrink will have one hell of a lawsuit on his hands if anything happens. You know, he's on probation, that shrink, for over-prescribing meds and also for self-medicating." She lowered her voice. "A girlfriend of mine says she sees him at the NA upriver."

Brutus sat quietly under the table. I listened to Shae but at the same time listened around the room to see if anyone was noticing the dog. Nobody was. Outside the window, Michael stalked by like a wizard, tall and lean. The hollows in his cheeks were grim in the bright morning sun, his Salvation Army coat long and loose like a cape, Mollybelle beside him. The cops watched him walk by too.

"Mick's out of it now," the first cop said, taking a bite of a sugary pastry; the sugar stayed on his mustache while he chewed. "They didn't hold him on that shoplift, put him away to dry out."

"Rough break, that dog business," said the other. "I'd like to get the sons of bitches that did it and cut off their balls."

Shae jumped in. "You really want to get those jerks,

keep your eye on Johnny Lul, lives up on Salsipuedes Road," she told him. "A friend of mine used to live up there, says he makes his dogs hang by their teeth off tires strung up on trees. Ties them on a treadmill. Sics them on other dogs walking by." The cops looked up at Shae and listened attentively, either because they knew Johnny or because they knew Shae.

"Up above the old water tower?" said the first cop. "I remember seeing some treadmills up there when we went in on a domestic violence. Might take another look, but the guy seemed pretty normal to me."

"Normal guys beat up their girlfriends?" Shae retorted. She finished off her coffee, then served herself a second, unauthorized free refill which she called "one for the road." She added sugar and milk and downed it, making a sour face.

I left the cafe with her and felt a flood of relief to be outside with the dog. I went with Shae to her car, but she had forgotten the marriage certificate, so we headed back to Garden Court. As we passed through the trellis, a man walking out stepped back to let us through. It was Johnny.

"What are you doing here?" Shae confronted him immediately. I felt cold sweat break out on my body.

"Hello ladies," he said not looking at Shae but past her, to me, to the dog. "I heard there was a couple empty cabins here, thought I'd take a look." Suddenly we saw management right behind him.

"Hey," Shae said to Marcuzi. "You rent to that scum bag, you're likely to have a lot more empty cabins on your hands."

"Fuck you too Shae," said Johnny. "My money's just as good as yours."

Management was trying to get out as fast as he could, trying to step around the little group of us but Shae put herself right in front of him, blocking him.

"I'm dead serious," she said to him. "You rent to that piece of trash that beats up his girlfriend and sics his dogs on other dogs as come by, I'm out of here. Consider this my notice."

"Well, Shae, now don't get riled up over nothing," management said. "Johnny here can't take the unit unless he places his dogs. I was about to mention to him that dogs aren't allowed in Garden Court."

Johnny looked pointedly at Brutus, close by my side. I could feel Brutus' body trembling but for the first time I wondered if it were fear or a silent growl. Management saw Johnny's stare and said smoothly, "This dog is simply being kept by our resident lawyer until a home is found for it."

"Well now," Johnny said, breathing out long through his nose and lifting his mouth in a line, smirking at me. "I guess I could help her with that."

"Get your bad ass out of here," Shae told him. "I know what kind of scum you are, and you better keep your nose clean at least for a while. I told those cops you had something to do with Lulabelle, and they're going to be looking at you real hard."

Marcuzi eyed Johnny again and it was pretty clear he had decided not to rent to him then or ever. Shae had guts, in-your-face guts, and if you could translate what she said beyond her personal sorrows, it had the ring of truth.

Management heard the ring of truth in Shae's words and so did Johnny and he pushed by her only muttering "bitch" as he passed close.

Marcuzi looked at Shae and sighed, then turned and left. Shae retrieved her marriage certificate and stormed out of Garden Court, yelling back after her a reminder to keep my door locked. I did as she said. I bolt-locked both doors and pushed the table against the one in the kitchen.

Late afternoon, Brutus walked under the table to the kitchen door, then stood, turning his head back toward me. He needed to go out, but I did not want to leave the cabin. Rage rose in me against him, fury at his need to go out, and the anger boiled over and fell hot around me. I kicked the mattress viciously and yelled at him. Finally, I calmed down. I knew he had to go out and knew I needed to take him, but it would not be very far or very fun.

I put on shoes and when Brutus understood. He bounded round and round, barking, and his tail knocked over the broom and I screamed at him. He pulled his ears way back, so his head looked round like a baby bird. I snapped on the leash, pulled on my coat and went out, bolt-locking the door behind us and putting the key in an inside pocket. On the way out, I passed Larry, walking up the footpath from the street. He would not meet my eyes. I asked if he wanted to come for a walk, but he said he needed to wait for his brother Harry, so I took off.

I marched grimly up to Safeway on River Road, then did a U-turn and walked back to the cafe, then around to Safeway again. A safe route, if boring. The dog needed a walk, okay, but he did not need to run and play. That's how you got into trouble, I knew that; playing and forgetting to look out for danger. It was not a day to take chances. But after a time, my anger settled. Brutus looked up at me with those gentle eyes, and I turned my steps toward the abandoned park.

Sunlight flooded the expanse of park. The ground still held the rainwater, so my feet sank in with each step, but I knew Brutus wanted to run, to leap into the air, to skid across the ground and bring me back whatever I threw for him. I squished my way down the path until I was under the apple tree.

Brutus turned circles in his excitement, tangling himself in the leash, getting me muddy, himself too. I finally unclipped the leash, then hastily reached into my pocket to be sure I still had the house key. I found it and it made me feel safer to hold it, so I clasped it lightly in my right hand, pressing it between my thumb and pointer finger. I could still hold the apple. I wound up and let it fly. It went a long way and Brutus tumbled over himself to retrieve it, then ran so gracefully back to me it seemed he was floating, up and down, like a wafted leaf. Again, I threw the apple and again it arched high and far before hitting the ground. It did not bounce on the wet ground but hit flat, still Brutus rolled and tumbled to get it, his life force awakened by the unexpected joy of the play. Over and over I threw the apple for him, then another, and another; I started slow but soon I threw with wild abandon, as though I had escaped something dangerous and deadly and now defied it, standing there in the sun of the late afternoon, throwing a plain apple as far as a shooting star.

Suddenly, a coldness occupied my chest, a terrible coldness, the same cold heaviness brushed through my body. I looked quickly in my right hand, the hand that had just thrown an apple as far as far. It was empty.

The hand was empty. The key was not there. I turned the hand over, looked on the back as if the key might be attached there, then looked in the left hand. As I did it, I felt the panic take me, occupy me suddenly, until the fear was everywhere and only the fear and no separate corner without it. I shoved my hands into my coat pockets, then into the jeans pockets so roughly I felt one rip. Nothing, nothing but my car key with my spare house key attached to it. The truth sank in slowly, that I had tossed the key out. When I tossed the apple, I threw the key too, the key to my safety, propelled it away from me in a high, soaring arc. The key lay in the field somewhere and anyone could find it, anyone could get in, get in and get me. The panic mounted, filling my soul.

Stop, I told myself, stop. Maybe I can find the key. The heaviness of my terror and despair lifted for a moment. Brutus felt my energy shift and stood a little off, waiting to see what might happen. I inspected the ground carefully all around me, not moving from where I stood, looking, bending down and searching, low to the muddy ground. Nothing shone in the sun, no glimpse of silver reflecting light. Maybe from a different angle. I moved back, up, around, watching for a gleam. There was no gleam and the sun moved inexorably behind the tall trees. I felt my breath coming fast, in, out, and the fear possessed me, entering me, blotting out the light.

I ran headlong down the path where I had thrown the apples. Stop, I repeated, stop. It could be anywhere along here. Stop this running, you'll never find anything. So I stopped and walked over it slowly, carefully watching each step of the way, eyes moving everywhere, step by step. Nothing. Only thick mud, rainwater in puddles, only dull puddles and dark mud and heavy grass. The triumph of my soaring throws was bitter now, a bitter taste in my mouth. Birds called from the trees, tee tee tee twerrp, a long trilling, but if they were calling to aid me, I could not hear them. I heard mostly a roaring, my eyes darting frantically. I had to find it, had to, anyone could find it, anyone could get in, he could get in. Who? I asked myself in fury. Who?

I caught my foot under a root and fell, hands and knees in mud. Brutus rushed to me and I pulled myself up, calming myself. Think now, think. It has always been your mind that saved you. Stop and think. Where would a key have gone had it been thrown with an apple? Farther? Almost as far? Halfway? It was lighter, would have been at the base of my hand, not in the fingers. There was no need to panic, I would stop panicking, I would do this scientifically. There was a plan. I would do this scientifically.

I stood up, wiped my hands on my pants, then walked back to the apple tree. My other house key was in my pocket, attached to the car keys. I detached it and palmed it. Then I found an apple, wound up and threw it, arching it down the path. I watched with all my attention to determine where the key flew. It fell earlier, I thought, yet still far down the path. I hurried over. Here, here it had fallen. No, there maybe, a little farther down. The sun dipped behind the redwoods and the ground before me was a patchwork of shadows, the mud, the shadows, the grass all of one range of color.

I searched calmly at first, then more frantically as it dawned on me slowly how utterly foolish my act had been. The chances of someone finding my first key and knowing it was mine, with evil intent, the odds of all that were so small, so very small. What madness had possessed me to throw the other key, the only spare in existence, to throw it down the path after the first? In that instant, I saw clearly that I was setting it all up, choreographing my own dance, and I remembered old Michael's theory, that we set up sorrows in our lives to recreate the sorrows we've forgotten, but the insight quickly gave way to the practical problem before me: both of the keys to my cabin were lying somewhere down the path in the mud, and there was not even sun to make them gleam. A flashlight, I needed a flashlight. I would go back and get my flashlight. It was, at least, a plan.

I forced myself to breath, in, out, then clipped the leash on the dog. As I turned to walk out, I saw three men walking in. I knew one of them, the father of Buddy, the man with the "No Fear" tattoo. All three of them stared at me. Had they seen me throw my keys? Not likely, not likely. And if they had? Nothing to be done, nothing to be done but stick to the plan. I passed them, leaving a good distance between us, my eyes withdrawn. I glanced back once, to be sure they did not stop to look for my keys. But they did not, they headed back into the forest and I hurried to Garden

Court. I would get my flashlight and go back. I would put Brutus safe in the cabin and go back. I had a plan and I held onto it to save my life.

I was passed under the Garden Court trellis when it occurred to me that I could not get the flashlight since it was in my cabin and I could no longer get into my cabin. The saving plan was without value, meaningless. There was no plan. I slowed my rush and walked now, feeling empty, light as dust. My mind turned this way and that, seeking a foothold, and I thought of the credit card trick. Of course, I had fixed my locks so that they could not be popped open. But maybe it would work anyway. Maybe I only thought I was safe but really had not been. I would try with a credit card. Only I did not have one. I went through my pockets again to make sure.

Suddenly a sound up the walk: Shae. She looked good, snappy. She waved both arms at me and I was never gladder to see anyone in my life.

"Hey there," she said, walking over. "Now this is what I call a lawyer. Ready to go after the shrink this minute for emotional distress. Says the bucks are there. They'd better be since he took two hundred big ones for costs!"

I asked her if she had a credit card. My voice sounded thin and squeaky, but she did not notice.

"No, I paid cash," she said. "Hocked my mum's silver tea service to pay for the costs," she said, lighting a cigarette. "Jerk at the pawn shop only gave me three hundred bucks, when he knows its pure silver, worth five grand."

I explained that I was locked out, without going into details. She finally heard me, and she pulled out her wallet and found a Visa card. "Try this," she said. "They've shut me off, so I'll be glad if it's of use to somebody."

As I took it, my hand trembled. I tied Brutus to the hose tap, not that he would run away but just to feel safe about it. Then I walked up to the door. I slid the card through, listening for the magic click, but I could not find it. I tried again, slipping the card smoothly against the lock mechanism but it did not give the clear pop I needed. Shae said she had another card and went over to her own cabin to get it and I took a couple of deep breaths to calm myself, then tried it again. The lock held.

Shae's cabin light went on and then I heard, "Oh my God." The card slipped through my fingers. I heard a bang in Shae's cabin, then: "Larry! Oh Jesus Christ!"

I ran over to her cabin and looked into the small room. Larry lay on the floor, naked except for jeans, a pill bottle open beside him. The odor of vomit hung heavy in the air, vomit on the dark rug, on his face. He lay on his back, his mouth open. I hurried over to touch him. His skin felt cold, but it was cold everywhere, evening coming on. I rolled him on his side to clear the mouth and the vomit tipped out and rolled slowly down onto the rug. The sight of it, thick, chunky, the smell of it, made me gag.

Shae sat at the table. "Oh God," she repeated. "Oh dear God." I looked at Larry's back, thin and pale. He had a tattoo on his back, just behind the left shoulder blade. It was a heart with writing in it. I thought it said "MOM" but when I looked closer, I saw that it was "SOS."

Suddenly, the body heaved, and more vomit ejected from the mouth. Larry gave a long, wracked sigh. Shae sprang to life. "Larry! He's still with us! Let's get him out of here!" Somehow we did, just the two of us, pushed up the body, and, one at each arm, got it out of the cabin, up the footpath; dragged it to Shae's station wagon up by management, wrestled it inside the car. She wouldn't let me go with her, just grimaced and shook her head. Then she was gone, tires squealing at the turn, gone down River Road.

Standing there alone on Fourth Street, I saw the moon rising. It was perfectly round, huge, a cold yellow, making its way up slowly as evening deepened. You could almost feel the pull, the power. It was the night of the full moon, the blood moon, the night of the eclipse. Suddenly I remembered that I could not get into my cabin. I remembered Brutus, tied to the hose tap inside Garden Court. I rushed down Fourth Street to Garden Court, hurried through the trellis, up the footpath. I ran to my cabin. Brutus was gone.

CHAPTER 22

HE WAS GONE. Gone. As if he'd never been there. Brutus was gone, his leash, his collar; his wide, trusting eyes. The hose-tap was there, cold in the moonlight. But Brutus was gone.

Blood pumped through my body, dousing it with the kerosene of adrenalin, lighting it with fear. Panic raged through me like fire through dry weeds, a dull roar of it, with little explosions as the different, horrible possibilities occurred to me.

"Brutus," I shouted. "Brutus!" I ran to Shae's house and threw on the porch light. No dog. Vama's was closed up tight, the veteran's too. Tony's old cabin was there, the door slightly ajar. I hurried toward it.

"Oh please God, please God," my mind chanted with each breath, a magic spell I had not invoked since childhood; but once again, no help was forthcoming. The cabin was empty. The train-roar of fear filled my senses, deepening into something else, an anger, a strength.

I stormed back to my own cabin and landed a kick on

the front door with all my force, then another. I knew my foot was hurting but I blocked it and kicked again, again. I heard a crack this time, a splintering, and the door flew open suddenly. I screamed, as if I expected a skeleton to be standing there, its bare jaw bones grinning. There was nobody. I flipped on the light switch and hurried back to the hose tap with my flashlight. Something was spilled on the ground there, something shining. I touched it with a finger, then ran into the cabin to the stronger light. Red, like ketchup. Red, like blood.

They had killed him. They had killed him right there where I had left him, tied up, unable to escape. I collapsed to my knees, forehead to the cold floor of my cabin. The frantic whirl and twisting of succeeding plans and fears slowed, like a play-yard merry-go-round when the class bell sounds the end of recess and the children run inside. My mind, abandoned by the will that powered it, slowed its turning, then finally came to a halt. Within me and without, silence fell over an empty courtyard. This, then, was the house of death, silence without stillness, the emptiness of empty hands.

Brutus was dead. On my hand was his blood, sacrificial blood. What sins had I committed whose forgiveness exacted such a price? Brutus, my child, I failed you, I failed once again.

I heard a noise behind me, looked up in an instant, filled with hope that it was Brutus, with fear that it was not. But it was neither hope nor fear there at the door, but the archangel Michael, appearing at my door in his Mickey Mouse sweatshirt, hood up, the full moon rising behind him, the full moon, pale yellow, rising just behind him, outlining his body with yellow light and casting his face in darkness. Still, I could see the eyes, eyes that had seen panic before and fear and loss, looking at me. He had come out to me, come out of hiding for me. He stood terribly still there, a stern archangel about to prophesy or render judgment. I raised my upper body, kneeling before him. Tears poured down my cheeks and I could not take a breath. Through my fault Brutus was dead, through my terrible fault.

"He's alive," Michael said. "They took him for the fight."

I breathed again, a long, sweet breath of night air. He was alive, still alive, alive again. In my mind, the battered body moved, turned, rose up. Something lifted me from the ground then and I was standing up, full of something.

"They took him for the fight tonight," Michael repeated. "Brutus bit Johnny deep, but they took him in the end."

"Where?" I asked, so very softly I was not sure I even spoke aloud. Michael said nothing. Fear flickered through me, an icy flame at the core, but I had no time for it. I shoved it aside and behind it, just behind it, was a different kind of flame, hot and dangerous.

"Where?" I spoke aloud this time, my voice ringing through Garden Court. "Where is the fight?" Michael shook his head slightly; he did not know. I stared hard at him, as if I could divine Brutus's location from the eyes that had seen him last, pick up the trail in those eyes and follow the bloody footprints. The boy stood like a statue, his face deep in the shadows of the hood, the full moon rising behind his head like a halo. Still as a statue. And suddenly I knew.

I was gone then, past the garbage bins, down the dirt alley. The abandoned park was a pool of moonlight, the bare apple tree casting bony shadows. The redwoods massed at the back, like a thick, dark curtain. I headed back, back, pushed through the curtain and into it, like pushing into a dream. The air felt thick, close; the path familiar. The moonlight sifting through treetops created an eerie twilight, and I could see familiar images as I passed: the arrangement of stones inside a burned-out redwood trunk, a fallen tree caught by another's branches.

None of it felt real. All of my senses were heightened in the urgency of the moment, yet I could not feel my legs moving, my feet pounding the ground. I was not there, was floating above, watching a girl run in panic in a thick, dark wood, a small body running. She was far below me, passing among shadows, yet I saw her clear as day, the lines of her face precise as a new leaf. A slight breeze in the trees seemed to whisper, and in the wind song, I heard the girl's voice, *stay, stay this time, I am afraid.* Her foot snagged on a root and she stumbled, fell. One knee hit against the sharp edge of a rock and the pain brought me back to the path and I pulled myself together and began running again. All around me the woods were deep and thick, each dark straight trunk doubled by its own shadow. I was there but not there, like in a living dream and it occurred to me that death would feel that way, past and present and future bound together only by moonlight. There were shadows everywhere, but my dog was at the end of the path; I trained my thoughts to that and nothing else.

In a moment, it seemed, I was at the top, approaching

the statue. There off the trail it waited, with its tale of darkness and of death, but there are things worse than death and I pushed on by, over the top of the rise. As I broke through the last line of trees, the scene opened up suddenly, illuminated by bright, pearly light. Moonlight lay everywhere, like a covering of new snow, making pale objects shine. The moon was high, huge, white, casting short, precise shadows. It was like a fairy tale, the moon so perfectly full, the eerie light, the shadows dark without a smudge, everything exactly where it was and nowhere else. I saw my own shadow on the ground, like the black-painted shape marking body placement in a crime scene. And down below, in the clearing, other shadows.

All this took an instant, just an instant. But it seemed such a long instant, as if my life could be lived in that instant, like the long last instant of the rabbit in hiding, waiting to see if the dogs would pass. I heard no noise during that moment, the stillness was extraordinary. The clearing might have been empty, liquid moonlight gathered in the bowl of land and redwoods, moonlight reflecting off the old church altar, the stump of the tree downed and stripped and violated so long ago, all silent as a graveyard. But it was not empty; men were everywhere. It was like a silent film, an old black-and-white film; figures of men moving about noiselessly, men pressing tight around the silent altar. Then someone turned on the volume and a wall of noise hit me and knocked me over like a wave.

Suddenly the night vibrated with noise, a rough mix of male voices, rooting, hooting, shouting. Above that was the squeak and static of a mediocre PA system, someone announcing, some music throbbing back somewhere, dogs barking; everything blending together indivisibly like smoke, and beneath it all, darkness, a darkness made tangible by the brilliance of the moonlight. It touched a sword of darkness planted inside me, an icicle piercing the very center of my heart, touched it and twisted. In that instant, fear made its move back in and I felt my hands tingling, trembling. I felt the strangeness coming over me, the distance, the dread.

Staying just inside the line of trees, I moved some yards off the trail, sank to the ground under a redwood. My entire body shook now, teeth trying to chatter, heart pounding. But I did not have time for it. I set my jaw, clamping the back teeth together, biting down the fear. It went down, but not far, just below the surface, circling there like a shark. It was enough, and I turned my eyes back to the scene below. I forced myself to look carefully, meticulously, as Columbo might have looked, absorbing every detail so that he could fit the last pieces together, testify to it later: the truth, the whole truth. Only by knowing the whole truth can a matter be adjudged.

The clearing was full of men, almost all of them white. I spotted one woman, a big blond selling beer and hotdogs at a table in a corner of the clearing. She drew a beer from one of the kegs, laughing about something. Several men stood near her table; others leaned over another table where money was changing hands. But most of the men crowded the benches around the old church altar where two pits were locked in combat.

The altar was shining. White carpet laid over the stump

glowed iridescent in the moonlight. A referee stood near the struggling dogs. The pits were locked together; one had the other by the neck, but its right leg was immobilized between the other's jaws. They moved very little, yet you knew something terrible was happening, like watching a tall building in an earthquake just before it falls.

I steeled myself to see Brutus, my eyes sifting through the images, but I could not find him. He was not in the fighting ring. One of the dogs was red with yellow over one eye, giving it a clownish look, the other white, almost silver in the moonlight. Dogs tied off the altar strained toward the fight. A brown pit bull lay dead to one side of the stump, a hypodermic needle still sticking out of its body.

On the altar, the silver dog broke free, but he was hurt, his leg completely skinned. The skin had been torn, then peeled down by the other pit, raw muscle and tendon exposed, blood everywhere. The dog tried to hide behind his owner in the corner of the ring, tail between his legs, as the clown dog came after it and the crowd roared.

The scene sliced through me like a long knife, ripping a hole in my armor. Fear rushed in though the gap and I closed my eyes tight to block it, but the darkness of my mind had its own rules. Out of nowhere, a series of images flashed through my head like slides, a crazy, living slide show: the ceiling of my old bedroom, corkboard with tiny flecks of gold; the small window, double-paned to keep out cold, the line of moonlight slanting in; my small fingers grasping my mother's arm so tightly that they had to pry them off when it was time for her to go. Big shoes approaching. Then a voice, a soft, silvery voice: *Come away, child, come away.*

I wrenched open my eyes and looked around shakily. I could see the full moon above me; below me, dogs were fighting, a different set of dogs, both yellow, one with spray-painted stripes of fluorescent orange. A cheer rose as the dogs charged across the ring and slammed into each other, blood spattering like ketchup. Blood stains on the carpet gaped like black holes in the shining surface.

Johnny was beside the ring now. He stood with another man, leaning toward him to make himself heard over the noise. Brutus was not with him; I could not see him anywhere though I looked until I thought my eyes would burn up with the need to see.

And if I did see him? What then? How could I save him? The newspaper said that the sight of an unfamiliar face was enough to break up a dog fight; the men would scatter into the woods leaving behind dogs and paraphernalia. They could never catch them with their pants down because the men took off running at the sight of a stranger. I only needed to go down.

But it can be dangerous for a little girl in the woods after dark. Fear drifted toward me like snowflakes falling though the light of a streetlamp at night, drifting down from way up high, closer, closer, until finally the cold kiss on your face. I felt the cold kiss of fear and I knew in that instant that I could not go down into the clearing, no force on earth could make me go. My dog was there somewhere, in enemy hands, and I could not save him. I would simply watch, like the others, when his turn came. Fear pressed heavy, now, like some cold hand holding me there by the throat, large calloused fingers against my throat. I could hardly breathe, and panic scattered my senses. My heart beat faster and I felt a slick of cold sweat on my back. I was trapped there, trapped, and terror began to descend over me but then I remembered a trick that I knew, a saving trick I knew.

Suddenly, down below, a buzzer rang, and reality cleared, and the round was over. The yellow pit was pried off, the painted dog dragged to the side by two men. Somebody turned up the music. It was Bad Moon Rising, and I thought of old Michael: *They couldn't kill it off, could they lass? Like a tree, with the strength inside. You can hack up the bark, cut off limbs, but the real strength is inside, the sap, the push to grow.* The tree behind me was a tall redwood; what counsel could it give me? I could see the soft bark behind me and above. It was fissured as if by sorrows, a thousand thousand years of sorrows, cracks etched the length of the trunk like dry creek beds. Fire had carved it; it was scarred deep and forever. But the tree was still there. I pressed my hands against the bark to ground me. A breeze rustled its upper branches in the moonlight, *ssst, ssst,* it seemed to whisper, *stay.*

Down in the clearing, two handlers brought another dog to the altar. Each had it on a separate lead, but they had to work to control it. I knew that dog, black, enormous, pitiless: the shadow dog. Fear mingled with a strange relief, as if I had been waiting for the shadow dog, waiting for this moment, all my life. The vet's father appeared near the altar, to the side; I saw him but had eyes only for the dog.

The set it on a bound cat and in just a few moments, cat blood was everywhere, overlayering the blood of the dogs whose turns had come before. Fear and phantoms mixed with reality until it was impossible to separate them, and everything seemed real and nothing seemed real. I heard someone call me–*come child, come away*. *Stay* said the tree, *stay this time, stay*, but the moon called me.

The men led out another dog to the alter, a smaller dog, eyes wide and liquid, ears back against its skull, its head round like a little chick. The moonlight turned its blaze silver, transformed the dark fur into deep velvet shadows. I knew him, knew he was trembling slightly, knew it inside of me without seeing; I had known this dog forever, since the very beginning of time. The moonlight shone down to me and fear spread out in a thick layer, suffocating me, throbbing within me and I remembered a trick that I knew. *Stay* said the tree *oh stay*. I always felt sorry to leave my sister behind, but I could not take her up the moonbeam, and as I went, I would see her small form there, on the blood-stained bed beside my empty body, her eyes wide and blank.

The dog knew I was there, felt it, sensed somehow that I was there. He looked straight up the rise toward me and I felt something else, something else inside. *Come* coaxed the moon, so soothing, so perfectly round and the tree felt rough now and though she spoke I could not hear her.

I saw Johnny then, leading my dog toward the shadow dog, and Brutus standing tall while the Shadow lunged toward him, almost pulling those two men off their feet; then the moon called and I knew I must go. I was sorry to leave my dog, but I could not take him up the moonbeam and as I started up, I saw his small form trembling, but there was the moon's round face offering me a way, one more time. I looked up dreamily, almost drowsily, to its reassuring roundness, but it was not round any longer, the moon was no longer round, an edge was gone, darkness appearing on its face, and spreading. The men looked up too and pointed and everything stopped, as the dark stain spread over the face of the moon and the light dwindled.

The dogs were taken down from the altar and tied to benches and someone brought out halogen lights on saw-horse legs, but they could not get them up and time passed, and more, and above us all the moon was consumed by darkness. It was like the end of the world, the light snuffed out before our eyes; soon it was almost gone, and it seemed all hope would vanish with it. But just as the last sliver of light disappeared into the shadow, just as the entire world was to turn into darkness, the whole round moon appeared again yet different now, red as blood, red as fire, and I felt something inside like fire too, a fire inside, heated, glowing. The wind roared in the treetops, no longer a whisper, but a call to arms, and the moon glowed red like lava, a whole moon consumed by fire and rage, and I felt the tree behind my back, its strength within, and I saw rising from the altar another tree, a tree like a cloud, tall as God and mighty and stern.

At that moment, the door of my memory split open and there was my father, the smell of his pipe, his huge calloused hands; his shadow falling over me. I knew in that instant what he had done; knew that he had tried to break me, that he had hurt us beyond healing. Rage rose in my veins like sap in the springtime and a scream came hot from deep inside me, not the scream of a child but of a warrior plunging into battle. I leaped to my feet and charged down the steps into the clearing, under the blood moon of early winter, the sea of men parting before me, men running, scattering before me; I rode that war cry down into the darkness to where my child had been waiting for me forever.

EPILOGUE

FROM THE LITTLE town to River's End, the river winds its way through low alleys, between rocky banks and grassy hillocks, now hurrying, now opening wide and slow, now sleeping with one eye open. River Road walks with it hand in hand as the river makes its final voyage to the sea.

Beyond the road are tall trees, the brown spires of redwoods, silent forests, slowly moving closer to the wide pale of the sky, closer to the ripples of high white clouds, high speaking to higher, the wind whispering through the very tops of trees, whispering of sun and rain, whispering of birdsong.

Approaching the sea, the forest becomes pastureland, the river solemn now as a child at the church door, face wide and shining. River Road can go no farther as the river spreads wide onto golden dunes. Here, the only sound is ocean wave breaking on a great beach where seals come to have their young in spring. It is winter and there are no seals, only great lines of seagulls rising and settling, white lines of waves coming in.

Larry died in winter. I walk down the narrow winding path to the beach. Dill grows everywhere, and her deadly sister hemlock. I carry one white rose, shining in the late morning sun, one long-stemmed rose, in memory of all that was lost, all that was gained. Brutus walks beside me, treading softly down to River's End to say goodbye.

Gulls turn overhead, white sails riding a slight, high wind, riding the back of sunlight filtered through the veil of fog. The sand underfoot has been washed by wind and sea into rows of small waves. Here is driftwood burned white by sea and sand, by time and wind, white now, some so light you can lift whole branches in one hand. Here are tree trunks white and bare as bones.

Shae will have a small ceremony here at River's End to scatter Larry's ashes. A dozen of us meet on the upper beach. Among the driftwood, we form a circle. Dunes rise between us and the ocean, but we can hear behind us the roar of the waves coming in. Someone speaks of Larry, his short life marked by the forever-sorrow, his fight and his surrender, and white seagulls turn and call and turn again as river disappears into sea. The tide is coming in, and ocean waves curve round dunes to meet river water. A counter-current forms in the very middle, pushing river water back in the direction from where it came, back, back for a last look, before curving round and descending to the sea.

Shae holds a photo of Larry, his high school diploma, and a box with ashes. When the talking is done, she leads us to the water's edge, to a small raft made of driftwood.

She places the photo on the raft, the ashes, the diploma braced up between branches like a little sail, and then she pushes it away from shore. The frail boat floats out toward the current. It trembles there gently, rocked by the waves, waves coming from the river to the right, waves coming from the ocean to the left. The raft wobbles there for just an instant, where incoming tide meets river water, then a breeze from the ocean fills the little sail and the boat begins a slow, march back toward the river mouth, rocking gently like a cradle. I see the photo of Larry, rocking to and fro, to and fro.

Shae picks up her bouquet and tosses the flowers, in ones and twos, into the water. Each one catches for an instant in the spot where river meets tide, then, surrendering to the ocean's slower, stronger power, floats on the current back up toward the river mouth, following the raft in its course. Soon Larry's little boat leads a procession of flowers, white and pink and yellow petals bobbing after on the swells. Then others toss flowers too, and each follows each, like gaily dressed girls following a casket; they trail the raft, winding back up toward land for a final curtsey, then turning and heading home to the sea.

I step out to toss my rose. I call up Larry's image, then let the rose go. Up up it flies, white as a pearl, so very lovely it breaks your heart to see, flying up into the pale sunlight, holding there a precious instance, then down in a gentle arc to the center of the eddy, long stem, soft head, bobbing on the tide.

Suddenly my dog is on his feet, running. Everyone turns, points as he plunges into the tide. Now he is in the river swimming, his little head one more point of light in the long procession of death. For many minutes I can only see his white blaze, bobbing there among the flowers. At last, he turns, struggling against the current, turns and paddles back to shore. He pulls himself out, dripping, shakes from head to tail, then races toward me. In his mouth is the white rose, wet, bedraggled. He carries it to me and sets it gently at my feet.

- the end -

ABOUT THE AUTHOR

Teo Spengler was born in central Alaska and spent her childhood there. She earned her J.D. at U.C. Berkeley's Boalt Hall law school, then headed to Paris where she worked as a documentary film writer. In time she returned to her native state and took a job in the Alaska Attorney General's Office in Juneau, suing oil companies. She is currently a writer and splits her time between San Francisco, California, and French Basque Country.

Made in the USA
Coppell, TX
28 January 2021

48925278R00134